A Smell of Onions

A Smell of Onions

Peggy Appiah

Longman Drumbeat

Longman Group Limited London
Associated companies, branches and representatives
throughout the world

© Longman Group Limited 1971

First published 1971
First published in Longman Drumbeat 1979

ISBN 0 582 64274.4

Printed in Great Britain by
Richard Clay (The Chaucer Press) Ltd,
Bungay, Suffolk

To Joe . . . with love

'*Aho ampam' gyeene*'
'Meddlers and onions tell
what's cooking'

Contents

Characters

Kwaku Hoampam	Farmer, shopkeeper, main character in story
Akosua	His wife
Kofi and Ama Serwaa	Kwaku Hoampam's children
Mammy Mansa (wife of K. Dom – deceased	Old lady
Mammy Mansa's girl	
Surveyors	
Mammy Mansa's friend	
Lawyer	
Nana Ababio IV	Chief of village
Nana Ama Gyata II, his sister	Queen Mother of village
Yao Afram	Linguist
Osei Kwaku	Farmer who breeds cattle
Kodwo Owusu	Farmer of cocoa and food crops
Kwasi Effah	Farmer
Wife No. 1	
Wife No. 2	
Kofi Asem	Small son of wife No. 1
4 Amankwa brothers	Farmers
Kwegir Bruce	Postmaster
Faustina	Postmaster's daughter
Yao Poku	Kwaku Hoampam's nephew
Kodwo Fom	Shoemaker, son of former slave
Adamu Lafia	Police sergeant
and family	
John Agyeman	Catechist
Kodwo Twum	Head teacher
Abena Ahoafe	New teacher
Kofi Ampim	Farmer and palm wine brewer
Osofo	
Odikro of Opepease	
Kofi, the catechist's brother	
Yao Nkrumah	Small time liar
Mammy Awuraa Ama	Old witch from Opepease
Kwadwo Oware	Thief from Opepease
Adwoa Ketua	Akosua's sister
Faustina's boy-friend	

1 *Kwaku Hoampam at Home*

The village is built on the hillside. The road crosses the stream and climbs the hill. No one can enter the village without being seen from the verandahs of the compound houses which lie back from the road on either side, but undoubtedly the best view of all is from the verandah of Kwaku Hoampam's house. It is just on the rise of the hill and at the point where cars and lorries must change gear before their last pull up into the village. There is a small shop behind the verandah and there, nearly every day, morning and evening, you will see Kwaku sitting in his rocking chair by the door, watching the road, a pipe or chewing stick firmly clenched between his teeth, or perhaps playing draughts with his friends or drinking a companionable calabash of palm wine, which he sells fresh and cool from the big pot behind the counter.

Kwaku has lived in the village all his life, as did his uncle before him. He owns several cocoa farms which are now managed by the children of his first wife and by his nephews and nieces. Their mother, may God rest her soul, died some years ago and Kwaku's second wife Akosua is an energetic woman in the prime of life. She has been to school and it is she who travels back and forth to the city to buy the goods for Kwaku's shop. She it is who inspects the cocoa farms and sees that her children go to good schools. They live with their aunt in town and only come home for the holidays. Kwaku is proud of them but does not interfere with their education—why should he, for is it not his wife who finds the school fees, pays for their clothes and only now and then asks for some money for shoes or hospital fees? She is a good wife and Kwaku is proud of her.

Once Kwaku himself worked on the farms; as a young boy he would follow his mother or his aunt when they went to weed the yams or grow the vegetables. When he was a young man he helped to clear the ground for the cocoa trees and to cut back the undergrowth which threatened to choke the young trees. He knew, in fact, every corner of the forest for miles around the village. He used to go hunting at night and his old gun still lay oiled in the rafters. But now, not needing to work, he has discovered the joys of being a man of leisure. Whenever his family tries to persuade him to go to the farm he sighs and says:

'Well, well, you see I cannot leave the shop. It is important that someone reliable should stay at home. You must learn to work out these problems for yourselves. When I die the farms will be yours.'

It is odd, however, that whenever anything goes wrong on one of the farms Kwaku seems to hear of it. Then he thinks nothing of walking four or five miles to blame a lazy worker, to threaten a neighbour who encroaches on his land or a timber contractor who steals or damages trees. For this reason Kwaku's family fears and respects him. They suspect that he has some juju—or perhaps the mmoatia, the little people, keep him informed.

The fact is that his eyes and ears are ever open and little happens in the village without his hearing or seeing it. He is as good a listener as a talker and has a way of getting information from people without their knowing it. His long, lean face is seen at every village occasion; he is called in to arbitrate in family quarrels. When he argues or expresses an opinion he is always two moves ahead of his opponent and can express himself in such a way that he can never be proved wrong even if he is mistaken. He has never been known to lose a deal over money or property. In fact he is a much respected member of the community.

Is he then not entitled to sit all day on his verandah and watch the world go by?

2 *The Old Must Go*

Some years ago, as our story begins, it was decided to put up a post office in the village. Kwaku was naturally the first to hear of it. The surveyors drove past his house and then stopped to ask the way to the Ahenfie. Kwaku slowly hitched himself out of his chair and walked ahead to the square in the middle of the village. He pointed out the Ahenfie lying on the left hand side of the road and was going to inform the Chief when the surveyors stopped him.

'We have to look at the house opposite the Ahenfie which used to belong to a Kwasi Dom, now deceased.'

'Oh! you mean Mammy Mansa's house,' replied Kwaku and took them across to a dilapidated house which stood in the corner of the square. The surveyors started taking measurements and Kwaku watched.

'Where are you from and what are you doing here?' asked Kwaku.

'We are surveying for the new post office,' said the older of the two men. 'That old house is to be pulled down and we are going to build a post office and telephone exchange in its place.'

'Where will Mammy Mansa go?'

'Mammy who?'

'Mammy Mansa who lives in the house.'

The man shrugged his shoulders. 'It has been sold,' he said. 'Perhaps she will live with relatives.'

'I must ask her,' said Kwaku and went into the compound of the house to look for the old lady. There was only a young girl in the yard and a few scruffy fowls. Only one room was properly kept and outside, sitting on the step, was Mammy Mansa. She was nearly blind and too old to recognise Kwaku until he spoke: 'Good-morning, Mammy. I hear you are moving. Have your nephews and nieces come to fetch you at last?'

'Is that you, Kwaku Hoampam? It is nearly a year since I saw any of the family. They don't seem to care about me any longer. No, I am not moving. What gave you such an idea?'

'There is a man outside who says the house is sold and they are pulling it down to build a post office.'

'Eeh!' said Mammy Mansa. 'Can this be true? No one has told me, no one has asked me. I am too old to move so they are working in vain.'

Kwaku went back to the surveyor.

'Mammy Mansa says she is not moving,' he reported.

'Is that my business?' asked the surveyor. 'I do what I am told to do and the rest can take care of itself,' and he went on with his work.

By evening when the workers returned from the farms everyone knew about the post office and the fact that Mammy Mansa was being made to move. She received so many callers that she became quite cheerful. Everyone offered sympathy and someone even brought in a few eggs and a little goat's meat to cheer her up. The young girl cooked it over the charcoal fire and Mammy chewed and chewed the meat with her old teeth whilst she listened to people discussing her move. She did not really believe it but it was good to have company.

But the story was true. The nephews and nieces had decided to sell—the building was central and they had been offered a good price. They did not want to live in the village in any case and the house would soon fall down. They reckoned they could easily persuade the old lady to leave and she would never know what happened to the house. It was not for two or three weeks that they came to tell Mammy Mansa that they had made arrangements for her to be looked after in town. They said they were worried about her being alone in the village and told friends that they were bringing her to live with another old lady who stayed next door to them.

When their smart new Opel passed Kwaku's verandah he heard the grinding of gears. When he saw the car stop outside Mammy Mansa's house, he hurried up the hill. Thus it was that he was a witness to the dramatic meeting between Mammy Mansa and her nephews and nieces.

It took a long time to exchange greetings fully. Chairs had to be fetched from a neighbour who, wanting to hear the news, also brought soft drinks and started to serve them busily. When the last grandchild had been discussed the young people came to the point.

'Auntie, we think you are getting too old now to be left on your own. We are worried about you so we have arranged for you to come and live with an old friend who lives next to us. In this way we can keep an eye on you and you can see the grandchildren more often.'

Mammy Mansa was shocked.

'What, leave the village, my friends and my house and stay with strangers in town! What rubbish, children. All these years you have left me on my own and now that I am dying you want to take me from my own home. Here I have lived and here I will stay until God thinks fit to take me away. I know all your tricks. You sent men to pull down my house without even asking me. Go back to your city. I have managed all these years without you. Leave me to die in peace.'

'But Auntie, we have sold the house. They are coming next week to pull it down and build a post office for the village. You must go.'

Mammy Mansa was angry. 'A post office, what rubbish. Here I live and here I will stay, in my own house, until I die. I am tired, children, and have had enough of this nonsense.'

She stood up slowly and without looking back turned and walked up the steps into her room. She shut the wooden door firmly behind her.

By now half the village had collected in the yard—the half that had time to stay at home and talk—and they were great talkers. The nephews and nieces found the argument taken out of their hands. It raged back and forth across the yard and there was no doubt that the consensus of opinion was that it would be cruel to turn out Mammy Mansa at her great age. They had done without a post office for the last—how long? They could wait a few years more.

Kwaku listened to the arguments on both sides and when the nephews and nieces at last had a chance to talk he was almost persuaded by their arguments. Did not the village need to be in touch with the outside world? If there were a telephone and a post office more people would stay in the village, the young would not be so anxious to get away; there would be more opportunity to trade.

'Why can't they build it somewhere else?' asked one of the women.

'This is the most central place,' replied one of the nephews. But Mammy Mansa's door remained firmly closed and the nephews and nieces were forced to leave. Kwaku heard one of them say to the others: 'We will send the bulldozer in next week. When the old house is down she will have no choice. What can an old lady like her do to us?' So they drove away in their smart car and peace descended on the village.

But not for long. Kwaku repeated what he had heard and the village was up in arms. Mammy Mansa was given no peace.

The whole matter was reported to Nana Ababio IV,

the village Chief, whose elders gathered in the centre of the village to discuss it with him.

It was evening and the oil lamps were lit and though the moon was on the wane it gave enough light for the villagers to pick their way unaided to the square. It is, perhaps time to introduce some of those who sat under the tree that night and discussed Mammy Mansa, her family, her life, her ancestors and the shocking behaviour of her nephews and nieces.

Nana Ababio IV was himself a very old man, so old that he had fought in the Ashanti Wars. The Queen Mother, his sister, was not much younger; under the stool name of Nana Ama Gyata II, she had supervised the women of the village for as long as they could remember and she knew every woman and child by name. Mammy Mansa was one of her oldest friends. Both she and the Chief were indignant at the news of Mammy Mansa's betrayal by her family. It is true, however, that they were almost more annoyed by the failure of the surveyors and the family to call at the Ahenfie first. Such things could not have happened in the old days.

With the chief were some of his stool servants, among them Yao Afram the linguist, almost as old as his master, whose completely bald head contained a wealth of information about the history of the village and of every family in it.

The villagers were mostly farmers, though as the years went by more people from the town came to settle there. Kwaku Hoampam was accompanied by his friends Osei Kwaku and Kodwo Owusu, two of the most prosperous farmers. Osei Kwaku had recently taken to breeding cattle which, inoculated against the ravages of the tsetse-fly, flourished under the care of a Fulani herdsman. Despite his success other villagers were slow to copy him, as they had been born and bred to the idea that cattle could not flourish in the forest area. Kodwo Owusu on the other hand had concentrated on his cocoa farm but now, more and more, turned to growing plantain and other food crops which he sent to town in his own lorry.

Kwasi Effah and Kofi Osei sat with the four Amankwa brothers—all farmers belonging to families long settled in the village. Talk went on late into the night but after a bit Kofi Ampim, one of the elders, signalled to a young man leaning against the tree, who left at once. Some ten minutes later he returned with a large black pot of palm wine, the calabash was fetched and conversation became more lively as it was passed round. Gradually people began to drift away, others nodded their heads; it was time to turn in for the night. No decision was taken other than that they would wait for something to happen. God was there and would surely see that justice prevailed. So nothing was done.

The next morning when Kwaku reported the night's discussions to his wife she replied indignantly: 'You men, that is all you do, you talk and talk and talk and decide nothing! You will let them take the house from Mammy Mansa. If I were not going to the city today to buy corned beef and milk for the store I would do something myself. I have to see to the children's clothes as well. Kofi needs a new uniform and Ama Serwaa has grown so tall that her school dresses are no longer decent. You had better give me money for the goods and add something for the children. You expect me to do everything.'

Kwaku seldom argued with his wife. He found her too useful and she spared him the tiring visits to the city which he seldom enjoyed except after the cocoa season when his pockets were full of money and he could buy what he liked.

He went into his room, unlocked the trunk under the bed and came out with a handful of money. They worked out prices and amounts and Akosua tied the money firmly in the cloth round her waist and took her bag, and when the early Mammy truck hooted outside the door she was ready to climb in and leave for the city.

3 *The New Post Office*

Later that week an old friend of Mammy Mansa's visited her house. He stayed talking for a long time and then Mammy Mansa untied the corner of her cloth and something passed between them. The next day a Mercedes Benz came to the village and drove straight to Mammy Mansa's house. Her friend and a younger man climbed out and went into the house.

When Kwaku reached the house to pay a morning call he found the young girl sitting with her cooking pot in the doorway. She smiled at him but she would not move from her place. Mammy Mansa had said that this meeting should be private.

Inside the house Mammy was talking to the young man and every so often he would write something down in the file on his knee. He stayed about an hour and went away again without anyone knowing who he was or why he had been. A few days later he came back, this time with an ink pad for thumb-printing and a long typed document. Mammy Mansa carefully wetted her thumb on the ink pad and pressed it to the bottom of the document. Her friend painstakingly added his signature. The young man went away and was seen no more.

It was Kwaku who saw the bulldozer come edging its way along the road to the village in the early morning. It bumped and rattled over the bridge and was followed by a lorry full of workers, with shovels and other tools.

'We have come to pull down the derelict house,' they said.

For once Kwaku hurried. He ran on ahead to Mammy Mansa's house calling as he went: 'Eh! they are coming to destroy Mammy Mansa's house.'

The farmers had already left for the farms and the square was soon filled with children and old people coming to watch what was to happen.

Mammy Mansa came to the door of the house and saw the crowd and the machines and heard Kwaku's cries.

'Over my dead body,' she said.

The workers were surprised. 'We were told the house was empty,' they said. 'Who is this old woman?'

'It is Mammy Mansa. It is her house,' replied the people.

The driver of the bulldozer asked the foreman to look at his instructions. 'It can't be any other house,' he said. 'The instructions are quite clear. We must go ahead as we were instructed. Perhaps the old lady is crazy?' Then he turned to the villagers. 'Someone take the old lady and her things. We will find where she belongs later. You villagers should look after your old people better and not let her wander around like this,' and he gave instructions to the driver to start pushing down the old part of the building whilst the other workers helped to take out the old lady's few possessions.

Mammy Mansa was not to be defeated. The spirits of her ancestors rose within her. She let out such a stream of abuse that the crowd was silenced. She pronounced a curse on all who should try and destroy her home—and then, and then, the effort was too much for her. She swayed on her feet and before anyone could reach her she collapsed there in the doorway and when they picked her up they found she was indeed dead.

There was a shocked silence. The bulldozer driver switched off his engine and mopped his brow. The workers trooped back to their lorry muttering beneath their breath. No one would now dare to lift a hand against the old building. The crowd parted and they drove away again from the village.

The news of Mammy Mansa's death spread through the villages. Relations who had not been back for many years came to arrange the funeral. The nephews and nieces came too, wearing orange cloth and weeping bitterly. They were not too sure of their reception but despite the slight coldness of the rest of the family and the villagers Death the leveller prevented an open split. It was a grand funeral, for all the village attended. Nana Ababio sat under his umbrella and danced to his drums. Nana Ama Gyata gave a big donation, wept and danced. The people came, celebrated and went.

The old house was left empty and the young girl went to stay with relatives. After the allotted time the relations met and were about to divide the property in the usual way when Mammy Mansa's friend arrived with the young man from town. To the consternation of the family he announced that Mammy Mansa had made a will — a thing unheard of in the village. When he started to read the will the faces of the nephews and nieces fell. This was not only a will but the expression of a determined personality.

Through the will Mammy Mansa proved beyond doubt that the house did in fact belong to her, along with the small farms worked by various relations in a nearby village. To her nephews and nieces she bequeathed a Bible apiece, hoping that it would do them good and teach them to respect their elders. To those who worked the farms she bequeathed the farms themselves. The rest of her property she left to her old friend the Queen Mother and to the girl who had looked after her. There were, in addition, instructions as to where to dig in the house for her family heirlooms.

The lawyer insisted that a pick and shovel be brought then and there and when the ground had been softened with water the family stood round as a hole was dug in the bedroom floor, beneath the place where the old lady had slept. They dug quite deep before they found what they were looking for: an old metal kuduo pot, its lid half worn away. Oil was brought and lime, and gradually the lid was eased off. Inside were old pieces of cloth and leather, and inside them a box full of gold dust, gold trinkets, a string of aggrey beads and various leather charms, so old that the skin was cracked and they had become a uniform dusty brown. The lawyer handled them carefully and asked someone to call the Queen Mother and the girl so that the things might be divided. Usually, this would have taken a very long time but the girl was young and the Queen Mother knew what she wanted. The girl was happy, indeed, to be given the gold trinkets and the Queen Mother took the pot, the beads, the gold dust and the charms. The few other possessions were soon shared out between them. The lawyer was asked to arrange for the sale of the house. The nephews and nieces left in anger and omitted to say that they had already taken money for the building; of how the matter was settled between them and the lawyer the village was ignorant.

Time passed; the village still needed a post office, so a year after the funeral the bulldozer came again with another driver. The old building, beaten by rain and unlived in, fell easily. The walls crumbled into the hole where the old lady's bed had been. Foundations were dug. The new building was erected, small, neat and white-washed with some rooms for the postmaster and his family behind it.

There was a grand opening ceremony and someone from the city came and made a long speech in English on the importance of progress and development in the rural areas. An officer from the Social Welfare Department translated the speech and the villagers clapped politely.

The big cars drove away, the people returned to their day to day occupations and soon the postmaster and his family moved in. The village forgot it had ever been without its post office.

In another year the telephone was installed. New buildings began to be put up on the outskirts of the village and the road was tarred.

Kwaku Hoampam spent hours watching the men working on the telephone wires until he felt he could have done the job himself. One of the workmen showed him how they tested the lines for faults and how he could hear conversations and listen in on the line. They drank palm wine together and became firm friends. The last day, when the workmen were ready to leave, some tools 'got missing'. They searched and searched in vain and since it was getting dark and the job was done they went away without them and they were soon forgotten.

Only Kwaku Hoampam knew where they were, under the old box in his house where his friend had sat to drink palm wine. 'They might prove useful one day,' he thought.

4 *Water and Music*

For the first few days the post office was very busy. People came in from the neighbouring villages just to see it and buy a few stamps. The telephone brought new interest. Kwaku decided to have an extension installed in his store; one was put into the school office; two went to the most wealthy farmers in the village; the other villagers used the box in the post office. The postmaster, Kwegir Bruce, was a middle-aged man who had long been a clerk behind the counter. This was his first post office and he was determined to make a success of it. He had no young family but one daughter Faustina away at secondary school, of whom he was very proud. She would come sometimes for the holidays but preferred to spend most of her time with friends in town.

Since the post office was not very busy the postmaster could afford to spend a good deal of time explaining how the telephone worked. One of his first visitors was John Agyeman the catechist who wanted to ring up the circuit minister in town. He came in in his old black suit, almost green with age and wear, and carrying a large envelope covered from top to bottom with writing. On it he had recorded the minister's telephone number. After exchanging news about parish affairs the postmaster helped him to put through his call. He spoke in a very loud voice as if afraid he could not be heard over all that distance. To begin with the villagers would ring up relations and friends in the city just for the fun of using the new phone, but after a bit they began to find it really useful as it saved many unnecessary visits to town.

Kwegir Bruce tried to make a small garden round his office but the goats and chickens and sheep of the village had other ideas. Despite the bamboo fence, nothing but the toughest shrubs survived—a few evergreens, a brilliant red bougainvillea and a sponge vine which grew on its own and climbed along the remains of the fence and up the side of the building.

Once there was a post office the village did in fact begin to grow. A few elderly people from the town built themselves small houses on the outskirts. Others who had cars or lorries and found it cheaper to live in the village and have their own vegetable patches also put up new buildings. The school was enlarged and there was talk of putting up a middle school as well. Time passes quickly, even in a village. Only the old Chief did not seem to change. Perhaps his skin grew a little drier and his eyes a little weaker. Many of the old stool servants died and it was hard to find younger men to take on their jobs; but Nana Ababio and his sister continued to watch what was going on and to arbitrate in village affairs.

Up till now the villagers had fetched their water from the stream at the bottom of the hill. It never seemed to run dry and when the village was small it did not get too dirty. With the growing population, and the washing of cars and lorries, something had to be done about the water supply. Other villages had pipes and wells so why should they not? Nana Ababio called a meeting and a delegation, including the postmaster, Osei Kwaku and Kodwo Owusu, the two farmers with telephones, and Yao Afram, the linguist, was sent to the city to ask for help. Naturally, Kwaku Hoampam was also included. The delegation was fortunate, for some of those who had come to live in the village worked in the Social Welfare and Water Supply Departments and showed them how to present their application. The village itself was prepared to put up some of the money. Kwaku constituted himself Chairman of the Water Supply Committee and before long there was a tap on a concrete platform not very far from Kwaku's store.

From his verandah Kwaku could see the people coming for water and watch the young girls as they did the washing or played with each other round the pipe. People coming for water would stop to chat for a moment or to buy a tin of fish or some kerosene or candles from the store. It was good for business and Kwaku was forced to take in a second room for his store. His wife saw to it that it was stocked with the necessary goods and she started trading in cloth in the store instead of going from house to house.

Kwaku's nephew from the city, who had been unable to complete school, came to help in the store. He knew his uncle well enough not to try and cheat him and under Akosua's excellent guidance he began to show a genuine aptitude for the business. Kwaku found him a great help as he could now leave the store and go and sit with the Chief when he felt like it. He never stayed away too long, however, as the view from the Ahenfie was not nearly as informative as his own.

Yao Poku, the nephew, was very fond of music and played the guitar well. He started to look for others in the village who had talent. Soon there was a small guitar band which practised in the evenings under a tree at the edge of the village. The young girls and boys would collect there to listen and to dance to the music. As the band improved it moved into the centre of the village. It began to compete with the Chief's own musicians in popularity and some people even employed it to play at funerals.

Do not think, because you have not met all the people, that Kwaku's household was a small one. The courtyard behind the shop was large and every room held one or two people. The kitchen in the corner was also large and something was always bubbling in the pots on charcoal fires. To begin with there was Kwaku's aunt, a very old lady who had stayed with him ever since her husband had been killed by lightning when working on the farm. Most of his own children by the first wife had moved into their own homes—either to be nearer the farms or else because their households had spread like his. One son, however, still stayed in the house and farmed the home farm with his nephew. His nephew himself had a large family and two wives who all lived in the house. Then there was Kodwo Fom, the son of a former family slave, who was now a shoemaker but had the right to a room in the house. He had several small children who were more like Kwaku than his own children and called him Nana along with all the others. There were other relations too whose relationship was too complicated to go into. All in all it was a very busy household and Kwaku found his peace as well as his interest sitting on his front verandah away from the cries of the children and the chattering of the women.

5 *The Lost Charm*

With the better road came more traffic. With the traffic came accidents. Drunken drivers caused quarrels in the village which could not be settled locally. Occasionally something would be stolen and the thief not caught. The nearest police station was a long way away—and so, inevitably, as the village grew, it needed a police station.

The police station was built at the bottom of the hill, not far from the stream. Until now the village had been pleased with its growth and improvements but the arrival of a police station brought a slight feeling of discomfort. Was not this something alien to their village life? Had they not managed their own affairs for as long as people could remember? They watched and waited. The building was finished and the small house for the policeman behind it. A telephone was installed and at last, one morning, a police lorry arrived with the family and possessions of the policeman. He came with help to unload the office equipment and to carry the things into his house. Thus it was not until late in the day when the lorry left with the other men that the village knew definitely what their policeman was like.

Kwaku Hoampam wandered down to the police station to look. He peeped through the door of the office and saw, bending over the desk, the solid blue-clad figure he was to get to know so well. The policeman sensed him at the door and turned round to see who it was. His broad face with its deep tribal lines showed him to be from the North. He was plump, good-tempered and middle-aged. Kwaku was relieved.

'I am Kwaku Hoampam,' he said. 'You are welcome to the village.'

The other man smiled. 'And I am Adamu Lafia,' he replied. 'I am opening the office tomorrow — tonight I am busy moving in.'

'You have come from town?' asked Kwaku.

'Yes, but I have been in many places and known many people.'

'I hope you will like our village. I don't think you will have much trouble here.'

'I hope not. I like a quiet place. In the city there is too much palaver — trouble if you do this, trouble if you do not, always people after you for this or that. You people don't know how lucky you are to be away from the centre.'

'When you have finished come and have some palm wine — my house is just there behind the store on the brow of the hill.' Kwaku pointed with his right hand.

'When I am off duty I will come. Thank you,' replied Adamu and went on with his work.

It was not long before Kwaku was able to talk about 'my friend the policeman'. Adamu liked to come and sit on the balcony with him. From it he could see his office door and anyone who came to the village. He soon learnt too that Kwaku seemed to know everything that went on in the village. He encouraged him to talk and gradually learnt about the village families, their problems and their characters. His knowledge helped him in his work and being a good judge of men he was able to have the maximum effect with the minimum of labour. Sometimes he would bring his two young sons Salifu and Ali with him, but his daughter Mariama stayed at home to help her mother. The two boys were enrolled in the village school and soon knew as much or more about the village than their father.

With the arrival of Adamu Lafia the people in the village began to remember their old grudges. Small thefts, long forgotten; differences over farm boundaries; quarrels over women. They all wanted to see and get to know the new policeman so they went to him with their complaints. To begin with he wrote them all down in a book. Once, after listening for two hours to the story of a robbery, he asked for the date and found it was an old complaint of some ten years standing. The man who was to blame was long dead and the complaint was being made against his nephew. He sat back in his chair and mopped his brow: 'You Ashantis!' he said. 'You talk and talk and trouble me too much. If you have a real complaint bring it to me. If not, keep your troubles to yourselves. Do you think that I am here to solve every family problem for you?' He closed his book with a snap and put down his pen. 'The next time you bring me some useless complaint I will show you what happens if you take it to town. Here you have me at your mercy but when you get to the city people are busy—proper—and you must wait.'

He discussed the matter with Kwaku in the evening. 'We don't forget easily,' replied Kwaku. 'Old quarrels die slowly. Before long you will know what is old and what is new.'

'I think I know how to stop it before then,' smiled Adamu. But he would not tell Kwaku how he would do it. His opportunity came only too soon.

Kwasi Effah, one of the village farmers, had just married a new wife. His first wife was not very old and he had already had five children by her—the youngest being a mere toddler, Kofi Asem, of about three years old.

One evening, as the women were talking with each other in the small market place, a lorry-driver stopped to buy some roast plantain. In pulling his money out of his back pocket he dropped in the road his good luck charm—made of red leather and fur—and when he climbed back into the lorry it lay there in the dust under one of the tables. Kofi Asem was playing nearby and pounced on this new treasure and started to play with it. When his mother took him home he had it clasped firmly in his fist.

Later in the evening, wandering round the compound, he went into the new wife's room and being distracted by a small mirror put the charm under the pillow and promptly forgot it.

That night, turning in her bed, the wife felt something hard under her pillow. She drew it out and held it by the small oil lamp on the shelf. She was horrified. Her heart filled with anger towards the first wife; she immediately thought that this was a juju put there to make her infertile or bring other harm. She started screaming and soon the whole house was awake. Before the husband could get there the two women were fighting and they had to be dragged apart before the tale could be told. The husband took the charm and looked at it. It obviously came from the North or from one of the travelling Hausas who dealt in such things. He did not think his first wife could have obtained such a charm, living as she did in the village. He sent the women back to their rooms and decided to look into the matter in the morning.

The morning brought no new light to the matter. No one took any notice of Kofi Asem when he tried to take the charm from his father, shouting that it was his. His mother spanked him and his grandmother, seeing how much he wanted the charm, was a little shocked: 'Eh! Kofi Asem,' she called after him, 'do you think you are a big man now and need juju?'

Since the family was unable to resolve the quarrel someone sent for Kwaku Hoampam. He came, listened and asked endless questions but no one could be proved to be at fault. When everyone had talked themselves to a standstill he went home. But the second wife was not content. She went in the evening to her family house and talked for a long time. She swore to bring vengeance on the family of the first wife. Her brother said he would see what he could do about it. A week later the brother went to the police station and saw Sergeant Lafia. He accused the nephew of the first wife of stealing the spare tyre from his lorry and brought a witness to swear that he had actually found it in the man's room.

This was the opportunity Sergeant Lafia had been waiting for. He phoned through to the city and arranged that both the accuser and the accused should be brought there. He also made private arrangements of his own.

The young wife's brother was delighted and he and his sister got ready to go to the city. The first wife decided to accompany her nephew as well and asked Kwaku Hoampam to go with them to help in the case. He went first to see Adamu Lafia and after his visit he told the family he was very sorry but he had had an urgent message from his most distant farm and would be away all day.

Adamu Lafia took the villagers straight to the Central Police Station in the city and found a bench for them to sit on. He went into the charge office and came back and told them everyone was busy and that they would have to wait. In the meantime he had other business to do but would return later. So there they sat all day. Whenever they asked when their case would be heard they were told that the officer was out, or busy. When it was getting dark they were told to return the next day. For three days they spent all day at the station. Both the men were anxious to get back to work. At first they did not speak to each other but as the hours went by they joined together in their complaints about the slowness of the police. The third day Adamu Lafia took them into the office and one of the police officers asked them about their case. 'Of course,' he said, 'such cases take a long time to investigate. Proofs have to be found and then there will be a court case and you will have to find lawyers. Lawyers cost!'

The two men looked at each other in dismay for neither could afford to spend more time away from work. 'You can withdraw the accusation since nothing is yet on paper—if you no longer wish to make it!' said Adamu Lafia, smiling. Both the young men immediately agreed. Even the wives, seeing what it would cost in time and money, forgot their quarrel for the moment.

When they returned to the village they complained bitterly about the police in the city, but, as Adamu Lafia had guessed, there were no more frivolous complaints. In the evening, when he went to drink with Kwaku Hoampam, he thanked him for the information which had enabled him to see to the bottom of the accusation and to deal with it appropriately. He returned to normal routines, the checking of licences, the investigation of road accidents and other day to day tasks which fill the life of a village policeman.

No one asked any longer where the charm had come from. But way up in the North, on a lonely road, the driver cursed the fate that had made him lose his charm. His front tyre had burst, the spare was punctured. As soon as he could get to Bolgatanga he would find out the man who had sold him the charm and buy another.

6 *Romantic Education*

At the far end of the village beyond the houses, in its own ground, stood the village school, ruled over by the head teacher, Mr. Kodwo Twum. Surrounded by shady trees and with a large games field to one side, it was one of the best schools in the area. Mr. Twum himself was a teacher of the old school, of the days when education had to be fought for and boys walked many miles for a chance to read and write. He was very strict, but was held in such respect by both parents and teachers that no one resented his discipline. He took a personal interest in all his pupils and was affectionately known as 'Master' by more than one of the big men in the city who had passed through his hands. The ground round the school was always well kept and tidy, for cutting and weeding the grass was one of the punishments given to inattentive or insolent children. A small farm belonging to the school straggled down the hillside behind it and the children were taught the elements of farming as part of their lessons. Master Twum's house was across the road from the school and next to that belonging to John Agyeman the catechist, so that the two men were often seen gossiping together of an evening, or going into the small village church to discuss parish affairs.

The church was built of concrete blocks, its woodwork faded and unpainted. It had a decayed air and looked half-finished. The roof, however, did not leak and the benches inside were strong. On Sundays it was packed by the villagers. They had always intended to paint the church but somehow it never got done. The building was adequate if unbeautiful and money was spent, instead, on buying an organ and in providing robes for the choir which practised two evenings a week, wet or fine. The choir was good and the Good Lord must have been pleased at the volume of song which arose from the church each Sunday morning.

On festivals, awnings were put up at the side of the church with benches underneath to seat those who were unable to pack themselves into the body of the church. Sometimes a preacher from town would come and take the service, christen the babies and administer Communion. The Osofo in charge of the area had many churches under his care and could not come often. The school teachers took the Sunday school and one evening a week the more devout members of the congregation would gather together to read and study the Bible. At times, Kwaku wished that he could read so that he could take a more active part in the discussions, but he would go and listen and think over the stories.

One evening he was standing on the bridge near the police station watching the water, strengthened by last night's storm, flowing swiftly under the arch. He thought of how the workman in the Bible had lost his axe and how Elijah had brought it to the surface of the water with a prayer. He wondered if the Osofo would be able to do the same—or the fetish priest in the village far along the road, who had a great name for his powers. Where were the prophets these days? Even the drums were silent and no message went from village to village across the forest. True, they played at funerals and the old drummers had lost little of their skill, but there was no longer a sense of urgency in their work.

Kwaku watched a snake swimming against the current. He bent to pick up a stone but the snake had already reached the bank and slithered off into the undergrowth before he had time to throw it. He dropped the stone and turned back to the police station. Adamu Lafia was busy eating his meal so he climbed the hill to his own verandah. His wife was sitting in the store but came out to join him and they sat together for a while, chatting about village affairs, about the farms and the children.

One day Kwaku was sitting in his rocking chair enjoying a pipe when school stopped for the day and the children started shouting in the street and making their way back to their various homes. Those from the family house greeted Kwaku politely before running in to change out of their school uniforms. Small girls, still in uniform, came to get water from the pump. One of the teachers came into the store to buy matches and kerosene for his lamp, bringing an old beer bottle to collect the fuel. He greeted Mammy Akosua and Kwaku.

'How are things?' they asked.

'Not too bad – though we are still short of two teachers. One new one is coming tomorrow and she will be staying at the Asante's house, not far from you. She has just finished training but at least she is fully qualified.'

'No doubt we shall see her,' said Mammy Akosua. 'What about the new middle school?'

'They have decided to build it at Bonsua on the main road. It is not far to the junction for the older children – little under a mile I suppose, and they will be able to use the buses once they get there.'

It was not long before Kwaku and Mammy Akosua met the new teacher, for she came to the store on her day of arrival. She said she wanted to look round the village and wandered in, glanced round the shelves, and asked a few prices. Had Kwaku been younger he would have whistled. For Abena Ahoafe was a very beautiful young woman. Her short-skirted teacher's uniform showed off her figure, her hair had been neatly plaited. She wore no make-up and her large dark eyes certainly needed no help. She started talking to Mammy Akosua, asking her about the village, where she could get this or that, whether there was a good seamstress—who made her own cloths. Kwaku tried to join in but she took little notice of him so he just sat back and watched. Mammy Akosua brought out her best pieces of cloth and garment and they discussed prices. Abena promised to come back and buy a half-piece when she received her first wages and asked if she could pay by instalments. At last she bought two tins of milk and returned to her lodgings to prepare her evening meal. Later she came out with a bucket to fetch water, but one of the school girls took it from her and followed her back to the house with the full bucket on her head.

'That's a nice girl,' said Mammy Akosua. 'I should think she will be a good teacher and the children will like her. Only she will have to be careful as she is very pretty—don't you think so?' Mammy Akosua smiled at Kwaku and went into the house to see about the evening meal.

Kwaku did indeed find Abena beautiful. He found her quite fascinating. He always enjoyed watching the younger women about the village but he had not felt this way for some years. He soon began to watch Abena whenever she went past and to get her to come into the store. He never bargained prices with her though he doubted if she ever realised that she was receiving preferential treatment. She was polite, charming—and distant.

There was another person in the store who took an interest in Abena. Yao Poku never pushed himself to the front while his uncle was in the store. Nevertheless he could look. This he did with ever growing enthusiasm. How was Kwaku to know that when he was out of the store and Yao Poku was in charge, Abena often lingered there chatting of this and that? She showed none of the reticence and shyness that Kwaku had noticed.

Although Mammy Akosua knew that Yao was interested in the girl, it never entered her head that Kwaku had ideas as well. She had offered to take Abena to the Women's Guild attached to the church and soon they were in the habit of going along together. They enjoyed each other's company and became firm friends. Mammy Akosua must have been some fifteen years older than the teacher but she found her a sensible and practical girl, who had received a good home training and seemed to enjoy her work. Sometimes when Mammy Akosua was in town or doing business for Kwaku, Abena came into the store alone. If it was evening and Yao had gone to practise with his band Kwaku tried to keep her talking, but she seldom stayed long.

Kwaku and Akosua had been married many years previously by customary marriage and though both were regular churchgoers they had not thought of having a church marriage any more than most of the other villagers. They were content as they were. Quite a number of the farmers had two or more wives and Kwaku could well afford to take another, but somehow he had never thought of it. Mammy Akosua had succeeded in fulfilling all his needs and he did not want quarrelling in the house. Abena made him wonder! He saw the way she walked in her short skirts. He felt that she must be approachable. He had not noticed a boy-friend with her. She was a wonderful woman.

One evening when Kwaku was out and Yao was leaning on the counter studying, Abena came into the store. Although Yao had not finished his schooling—largely owing to bad teaching in the school he attended—he was an intelligent young man. He tried to go on with his studies in the evenings and read anything he could lay his hands on. He was one of the most faithful users of the Library van. When Abena came in, he looked up and smiled. He closed his book and asked what he could do for her.

'What are you reading?' she asked.

'Oh! just one of my old school books. I never had a chance to take any exams but that does not stop me from wanting to learn. The trouble is that it is so hard to get anything to read.'

'Why don't you come and see what I have?' replied Abena. 'Perhaps I could help you. You know you can still work for your 'O' levels at home and even if you don't get them you will learn.'

So Yao started to visit Abena and to make use of the few books she had. They enjoyed working together and Abena came to respect Yao's intelligence and to wish that he had had further training.

Of all this, curiously enough, Kwaku heard nothing. I suppose he took his nephew for granted. It is often easy to miss what is going on right under your eyes when you are interested in everyone else's affairs.

One day when Abena came into the store and found Kwaku on his own she was about to hurry out when he called her: 'You are a beautiful girl,' he said. 'Aren't you thinking of getting married?'

'Whoever to?' she asked surprised. When Kwaku started talking of his own position in the village and how well he looked after his family, she realised her mistake. She was angry and annoyed. Could not the old man realise his age? He had a good wife. He had grandchildren. He could not possibly believe that she would be interested in him. She hastily bought a tin of sardines and hurried from the store.

From that time she was very careful only to go into the store when Yao or Akosua were there. But she and Yao continued to meet outside. Abena had a pleasant singing voice and sometimes she would wander up to listen to Yao playing his guitar. Soon, with other young men and women, she formed a small singing band and she and Yao would sing duets together, accompanied by his guitar. Their voices were well matched.

By now Yao was very much in love with Abena but he dared not ask her to marry him. He depended on his uncle for his keep and though he had a fairly generous allowance it was not enough to support a family. Abena realised his dilemma. She had a job and a training and she did not see why she should not marry him. She was sure that, in time, he would be able to pass his exams. Then he could go to Teacher Training College and they could work together at some school.

Months went by and Yao said nothing. Abena taught him all she could. She thought that, if he could get two or three months good teaching, he might now be ready for his 'O' levels. But he must devote his whole time to working. She would have to speak to his uncle. She waited for an opportunity.

Kwaku had almost given up hope that he would get Abena to himself again and was surprised when she came straight into the store one day. 'I have wanted to speak to you for a long time,' he said, 'but you never seem to be on your own.'

'I, too, wish to speak to you alone,' replied Abena. Kwaku felt more hopeful.

'It's about Yao . . .'

'About Yao?' asked Kwaku, puzzled.

'Yes, he and I have been studying together. He is very clever, you know. I think he is almost ready to take his 'O' level exams, only he needs a good teacher and two or three months of full-time study.'

Kwaku looked as surprised as he felt. Not only had he no idea that Abena knew his nephew well, but he had never considered Yao as being clever.

'Why are you so interested?' he asked.

Abena felt that she must take the bull by its horns. 'I would like to marry him,' she said. 'If he can go to

Teacher Training College, then we can both work together.'

Kwaku was, by now, unable to hide his consternation. 'Marry Yao!' he exclaimed. 'Did I hear you say, marry Yao?'

'Yes, of course.'

'Has he asked you?'

'No, he does not like to until he finishes his education. But I know he wants to marry me.'

'I've never heard of such treachery!' said the outraged Kwaku. 'I must speak to the boy. I had thought better of him. How dare he—and without asking me?'

'Why on earth is it treachery?' asked Abena, angrily. 'Don't you like me? I always thought you took an interest in my welfare, the way you look at me and talk to me in the store! And Mammy Akosua is a friend too!'

'Of course I like you,' said Kwaku, on firmer ground. 'In fact I love you. You would be quite wasted on a small boy like Yao!' He pulled himself up: 'Why, I had thought of asking you to marry me, myself.'

'What?' cried Abena, now thoroughly angry and caught off balance. 'I would rather die than marry an old man like you.' She ran out of the store in tears.

The whole interview had been a shock to Kwaku. His pride was bitterly hurt. Then he was furious with his nephew. How could Yao have done this to him after all the help he had been given? He was so confused that he needed time to think. He closed the doors of the shop, put on the padlock and retired to his room. An old man indeed! A man was as young as he felt. Mammy Akosua would never have said that to him—no never. Now she was a sensible woman. Kwaku began to think of Mammy Akosua. He was used to asking her advice. Unable to decide how to punish Yao, he decided to consult her.

When Abena ran out of the store she was very angry. When she had had time to think, she realised that she might have done great harm to Yao. She had not asked him before going to his uncle. He would have to be warned. She knew that he had gone to town with Mammy Akosua and would soon be home. She went straight to the bus stop to wait for them. As she waited she thought of what she should do. Yes, Mammy Akosua was the only one who could help.

As soon as the bus stopped Abena looked anxiously at the passengers. Then she spotted Yao who was helping Mammy Akosua to collect her parcels. Soon they were out of the bus and starting towards the house.

'Stop! Please stop,' said Abena. 'I must talk to you before you go home. Please, it is very important.'

Mammy Akosua looked at her in surprise. 'What is the matter? Has there been an accident? Why are you crying?' Then she turned to Yao: 'Take these parcels to the house and tell them I am just coming,' she said. 'I am going home with Abena and you can join us later.'

As soon as they were in her room, Abena told Mammy Akosua all that had happened. She was too upset to think of the effect it must have on Kwaku's wife. Mammy Akosua listened in silence. When Abena had finished she burst out angrily: 'These men! When will they see sense? But you should never have said that to Kwaku. It doesn't do to hurt a man's pride. Still, I suppose he deserved it. We shall have to think what to do.' She sat silent for a minute while Abena dried her tears. She was glad that the older woman was not too angry. Then Akosua smiled at her. 'You would make a good wife for Yao. He needs someone to make him work. We shall have to see how we can manage it.' Akosua laughed. 'I can just see Kwaku's face when he hears that I know all about it. Maybe it is a good thing after all. Leave it to me.' At that moment Yao returned and Akosua soon left for home, leaving the young people to themselves.

No one else was present at the interview between

42

Mammy Akosua and Kwaku. But Yao soon went to town to find a good teacher and to take his exams. Kwaku promised that, if he passed, he could marry Abena. Akosua definitely had the upper hand. But she was a very tactful woman and she so spoilt Kwaku that after a bit he began to consider himself fortunate that he had not taken on a second wife.

Time passed. The exams were taken. Yao came home to wait for the results. He spent a miserable two months waiting. He was sure he had not passed and Abena had to work hard to keep up his spirits.

When the letter finally came, Kwegir Bruce the postmaster, knowing how long Yao had been waiting for it, brought it straight to the store. Kwaku was almost as excited as Yao. The envelope was opened. Yao unfolded the paper and then gasped. He had passed four out of the five subjects he had taken, the way was open. He could go to college.

As soon as school was over that morning, Yao met Abena. She saw his face.

'Have you heard?' she asked, hardly able to hide her excitement.

'I've passed,' he said.

'Praise the Lord. I knew you would. Now we can get married.' There were no two happier young people in all Ashanti.

In the evening they went to see Kwaku and Akosua to discuss wedding plans. Abena's mother was long dead and her father had married again, so Mammy Akosua was determined that the wedding should take place in the village. She had other reasons as well.

When they were alone that night, discussing plans, Akosua turned to Kwaku. 'I think we had better get married in church too!' she said. 'I will arrange for us to be married at the same time. Tomorrow you and I will go and see the priest. I don't want you to be tempted again.'

What could Kwaku say? He could not afford to have the village know that he had been refused. The whole village would laugh at his being called an old man. He knew there was no point in arguing. 'Perhaps we had better,' he said. Later, as he lay awake, he thought and thought. He became more and more filled with admiration for his wife. What other woman could have managed as she had done, could have taught him a lesson so discreetly and without jealousy. 'What a fool I was,' he thought, 'married to such a wonderful woman and not realising it.' Few people in the village would have credited him with such frankness. But it is easier to be honest when alone and when one's reputation is not at stake.

The next day Kwaku and Akosua went to visit John Agyeman to ask when the Osofo could come to the village for the wedding. The catechist was sitting in his room fussing over the church accounts. Usually 'Master' helped him, but this week he had been away at some conference in town. Kwaku greeted the catechist and then hesitated. Akosua stood smiling behind him.

'The fact is, John,' said Kwaku, 'Yao Poku and Abena Ahoafe have decided to get married. We want to have the marriage here as her mother is no longer alive. What is more, Akosua and I have decided to get married in church at the same time.'

John could hardly hide his surprise. That the young people should be marrying was natural — such things happened daily. That Kwaku and Akosua should want a church wedding after all these years was, however, a shock. Perhaps the young people had made them feel sentimental? Not knowing quite what to say, he dropped his pencil, bent over to pick it up and then smiled.

'Congratulations,' he said. 'And when will the happy event take place?'

'That is what we came to ask you. We don't know when the Osofo comes again. We would like it to be at

Easter, if possible; then everyone will be on holiday.'

'It would give us time to prepare,' said Akosua. 'I must have the dresses made and invite the relations.'

John scratched his head. 'I shall have to consult the Osofo. Of course such a wedding is an important occasion and we might persuade him to come. Perhaps I could visit him and see?'

'Akosua will be going into town tomorrow and will accompany you if you are free,' said Kwaku.

'I would be grateful if you could manage it,' added Akosua. 'I know Adwoa Ketua would be pleased to see you if you could spare time to visit her too. We could have lunch there before returning home, and discuss it with her and the children.'

John Agyeman decided that the accounts would have to wait a bit longer and that the schoolchildren could do without their instruction for one day. He gratefully accepted the offer of a free trip to the city and a meal at Adwoa Ketua's, who was well known for the quality of her fou fou and abenkwan (palm soup).

In the evening 'Master' Twum returned from his conference and came to sit with his friend and discuss the events of the day. John told him about the forthcoming wedding. He was as surprised as his friend. 'Well, well,' he said, taking off his glasses and polishing them with the corner of his shirt. 'I wonder what has made him do that? Kwaku Hoampam is the last man I would have expected to make such a decision. He is too cautious a man to make it lightly—and why now, after all these years? Something must have happened to make up his mind; but what?' Although they discussed the matter late into the night neither John nor 'Master' could think of a reason why Kwaku should get married in church.

At Easter the Osofo found time to visit the village and the grand marriage took place. Akosua, determined to have a full white wedding, had offered to provide both the dresses. Abena, anxious to please the family—for Yao had to have some support until he had finished his training, agreed to let her organise everything.

Thus on the wedding day the two brides were dressed alike, even to the bouquets of artificial flowers, ordered specially from Accra. But, whereas Kwaku appeared in Kente, firmly refusing to put on a dark suit for the first time in his life, Yao was dressed in a suit of the most modern style and wore a white flower in his buttonhole. There were a multitude of little bridesmaids in blue frilled dresses. Abena's father, relieved at not having to do anything for his daughter other than to be present, arrived with his wife and a gold necklace for the bride.

All in all it was a wonderful wedding. The village talked of it for years. Drinks flowed freely, cakes were distributed to the children. The young couple went off to Cape Coast for their honeymoon, in a borrowed car. When the last guest had gone, Kwaku and Akosua retired exhausted to their room. The whole thing, though costly, had been a success and they were satisfied.

The villagers, like their teachers, remained puzzled. They never could understand why Kwaku and Akosua had suddenly decided to get married—and unless the story leaked out, they never would. It was one of those things!

7 A Policeman's Dilemma

One character in the village puzzled Adamu Lafia. He was that quiet wisp of a man Kofi Ampim. He was a regular churchgoer and an elder of the church and yet he seemed to be popular with even the wildest young men in the village. Although he seldom smiled they all treated him with affection and respect. Adamu learnt that he was a farmer but saw no evidence of his farming. People came and went from his house, particularly in the evenings.

One day when Adamu was sitting talking with Kwaku outside the store, Kofi Ampim went past, walking hurriedly up the hill and scarcely pausing to answer the greetings which followed him through the village.

'Who is this man Kofi Ampim?' asked Adamu. 'He is such a dry stick of a man and yet everyone seems to know and like him. I have never seen him smile.'

Kwaku thought a moment, wondering how much he could tell his friend. If he did not say anything, that in itself would be suspicious, but he thought it better that Adamu knew as little as possible about Kofi.

'He's an elder of the church and never gets drunk at funerals,' he said at last. 'His uncle was one of the founders of the church here and his wife is related to Nana Ama Gyata.'

'Yes, but what does he do?'

'Oh, he has a farm. It is mostly worked by the younger members of his family these days. He is a good man.'

'Why is he so popular?'

'He never harmed anyone.'

'Yes, but is that enough?'

Kwaku grew annoyed. 'I can't tell you all about everyone in the village,' he said. 'You had better ask someone else.'

Adamu was surprised at his reaction and wondered what he was hiding. He thought he had better investigate for himself.

Thus it was that Adamu took to wandering up to the other end of the village each evening and gazing at Kofi's hut, which stood on the very edge of the village. Behind it a well-worn track led into the bush.

Now the villagers were quite aware that Adamu was watching Kofi's house and they warned the old man. They also set up a watch system of their own. Whenever Adamu drew near, pots and bottles were quietly set down on the ground and people went innocently to and fro and greeted the policeman as they passed. One evening Kofi called to him to come in and he sat and chatted in the courtyard of the house for some time whilst Kofi's grandchildren stared at him with big eyes. But he was still not satisfied.

One afternoon he went up to the school playground and looked around. He saw a friend of his son's, a rather round-eyed small boy known as 'Kuku'—though no one knew why.

'Kuku,' he called, 'I have an important message for Kofi Ampim, can you take me to him?'

Kuku looked at him, puzzled, but he saw that he was friendly and smiling. It could do no harm.

'He does not like people visiting him at work. He is busy in the afternoons.'

'This is important. Where can I find him? I will give you a penny if you tell me.'

Adamu held up the penny. Since everyone in the village knew where Kofi was, Kuku could see no harm in taking the policeman there. He held out his hand for the penny.

Together they set out along the forest path. It branched quite frequently but Kuku seemed to know the way well. He trotted along the path until they came to a barrier of thorns, put there apparently to block the way. Kuku turned to the right, doubled back and soon, after several twists and turns, came back onto the path at the other side of the barrier. There he stopped and put his finger to his lips.

'I had better go and ask him if he can see you,' he said. 'Wait here,' and he trotted on along the path. But Adamu did not wait, he followed quietly behind the small boy. Thus it was that he reached the illicit still before Kofi or anyone had time to cover up signs of the work. Big black pots of the already prepared drink stood by the entrance and inside Kofi whistled away happily at his work. 'Uncle Kofi,' called Kuku, 'someone wants you.'

'Coming,' said Kofi and came out of the shelter wiping his hands. When he saw the policeman he gave a gasp of dismay.

'So-oo,' said Adamu. 'I wondered what you were up to!'

'It does not do any harm,' stammered Kofi. 'We have always made it here – I and my uncle before me. It keeps the village happy and supports the church. Isn't that how we got the new roof, and now we have nearly paid for the organ.' He waited for Adamu to reply. Adamu was confused. Had he known what was happening he would probably have steered clear of the place, or told them he was coming. Now Kofi had been caught red-handed and he would have to do something about it.

'You know it's illegal, I suppose,' he asked hopefully.

Kofi took his cue. 'Goodness me! Is it really?' he asked. 'I never knew! We have done it for generations and no one has ever complained.'

Adamu smiled. 'I shall have to warn you,' he said solemnly. 'I will come back in a week's time and unless all trace of the still has gone I shall have to report the matter to Headquarters.'

'Now I know it is illegal, of course I will stop,' replied Kofi. Adamu thought he heard him chuckle. He turned round and calling Kuku, went back along the path.

That evening Adamu sat with Kwaku again, drinking palm wine: 'Your friend Kofi Ampim is a man of parts!' he said to Kwaku.

'What? Er—yes,' said Kwaku, with a question in his voice.

'Is there anyone in the village who does not know what he does?'

'What do you mean?'

'Where does the village get its drink from?'

'So you know!' said Kwaku. 'What are you going to do about it?'

'What do you suggest?'

Kwaku looked at his friend. 'What did you tell him?' he asked.

'I said I would go back in a week and if the still was not destroyed I would report it! Of course, he said he had no idea that it was illegal. I forgot to ask him why there was a barrier across the path.'

Kwaku chuckled and looked at his friend appreciatively.

'That's all right then. Why don't you arrange to inspect the area each week—say on a Monday. Then things can be arranged. You won't find it again.'

Adamu smiled. He knew well enough that if he reported the still he would earn the undying enmity of the village. He sympathised with the villagers, for did not his own uncle own a similar still in the North? There was little chance of anyone else reporting it and he could always plead ignorance. So he came to an agreement with his own conscience. Each Monday he went into the forest and looked at the place where the still had stood. Sometimes he was accompanied by old Kofi himself, but gradually the path became so overgrown with shrubs and weeds that the visit scarcely seemed necessary. He carefully forbore to look along the other paths, for how could he be expected to know which farms they led to? So, instead of visiting the forest he took to dropping into Kofi's house for a glass of fresh palm wine. They became good friends and Adamu discovered that underneath the austere exterior Kofi had a nice dry sense of humour and a great fund of knowledge about the village and all that went on there.

8 *The Great Robbery or, 'Ever Been Had?'*

Newspapers seldom reached the village before the afternoon when the mammy lorries began to bring people back from the city. Kwaku usually went down to the police station in the late afternoon when Adamu Lafia studied the daily papers. He read them from cover to cover 'in the course of duty'. It was, in fact, necessary to keep an eye on the papers for official circulars often took long to reach the village and one could not listen to the radio all the time. Sometimes laws would be changed, the numbers of wanted cars would be published, news of local robberies given. It was as well for a policeman to know what was going on. It was also a help to discuss these events with someone else.

From being an expert on village affairs Kwaku, therefore, became something of an expert on affairs of state. Unfortunately, he had not the knowledge or background to understand a good deal of the news. Nontheless he had views on almost everything. He was much influenced by the editorial opinions in the papers and disagreed with them only when their opinions violated the tenets of local custom and the accepted moral standards of village life.

Perhaps the most difficult thing to understand was the lack of arbitration in international affairs. Being unable to picture the historic background and the importance of political beliefs, he found it difficult to understand why the countries who always shouted, 'We want peace,' should always be at war with each other! Why could they not submit their cases to normal arbitration and decide them on a basis of give and take? He thought of the many cases of boundary disputes which Nana Ababio had settled over the years, of the long discussions when this or that stream changed its course, when a boundary tree fell, struck by lightning, or when families divided up the farms between them. It was perhaps lucky that the pictures and horrors of modern warfare had little reality for him as he could scarcely realise such devastation from his limited experience.

The stories of local robberies were easier to understand. He strengthened the locks on his own store and made sure that he always had a good dog in the house; although, in truth, he doubted the ability of any thief to break in in the silence of the village night when all the dogs were on the alert. His house was near the centre and he felt quite safe.

One afternoon he sat with Adamu in the police station just after the newspaper had arrived. Adamu was absorbed in a story on the front page of the local paper.

'Ayee, ayee, what will happen next?' he said.

'What has happened already?' asked Kwaku.

'The lorry of the Bulco Timber Company has been held up near Bonsua on the main road. The driver has been knocked out and the month's wages stolen. A farmer on his way from the farm saw a blue Peugeot car driving at furious speed from the direction of the hold-up. Someone else saw the car driving along this road . . .'

Adamu looked up. 'Did you see it, Kwaku?' he asked.

'Yesterday I was on my farm,' replied Kwaku, regretfully. 'I will ask the children of the house. Why don't you question the other villagers. Someone must have seen it?'

So Kwaku went back to his house and asked if anyone had seen a blue car coming through the village. They all shook their heads. Adamu, too, asked all the people he knew to have been about at the time. No one had seen the blue car.

It happened that the postmaster's daughter, Faustina, was home on holiday. She had stayed with her friends in town as long as possible but her father would give her no money whilst she was away from home, so she was now forced to stay in the village. She was lonely and she was bored. She helped her mother with the cooking and her father with the office, but there was still time to spare. The bright spot of the day was when the telephone rang in the evening and her friends spoke to her from town. To her mother she said: 'It is just Justina—she wants to know how I am,' or, 'Mary wants me to spend the evening with her and go to the cinema.' But it was not the voices of Mary and Justina she listened for but a certain deeper one. Mary and Justina knew all about it for was it not a 'brother' of Justina's who phoned? He met her often in town, he was attentive and affectionate. She was nearly nineteen. Village life was indeed boring.

Kwaku had noticed that nearly every evening Faustina went to the telephone box. If anyone else wanted to telephone they had to wait. He wondered what she could be doing—surely she was too young for business or family affairs. When he asked her father he just laughed and said: 'She is young and these schoolgirls have many friends.' He was proud of her popularity.

It was not until the blue Peugeot came to the post office that Kwaku became really curious. It arrived one evening with two young girls. The driver and the girls got out and went in to call on Kwegir Bruce and his wife and presently Faustina came out, all 'kama kama' in her best cloth. She got into the car and drove away.

According to the papers the police were still looking for the blue car. It had started along this road to the village and apparently disappeared. Yet here was another blue Peugeot coming to the village post office. Could it be the same? Kwaku had forgotten to ask the number of the missing car.

Kwaku had forgotten the tools that the telephone man had left behind, but that evening when he was cleaning the store, he found them tucked away in a corner. He wondered if he would still know how to use them. It would be amusing to try. For two days he wavered. On the third evening he told his wife he was going for a walk as far as the junction to see his friend at the petrol station. He took a small bag with him and set off just as it was getting dark. If he had timed it right, Faustina should get her evening call just after he reached his goal, and he could satisfy his curiosity.

It was not to the junction that Kwaku went, he followed the road as far as the big curve that avoided the marsh. Then he took the broad track which followed the telephone poles when they took a short cut across the bend. As soon as he was out of sight of the main road he found the pole he was looking for. For some reason or other the broken-off trunk of a large tree had been left alongside the pole and Kwaku knew that if you climbed up carefully you could reach the wires. Perhaps it was for this reason the trunk had been left. He was remarkably nimble for his age and was soon sitting on the top of the trunk. It was as well that he had really watched the engineers. He took out the tools and carefully 'fixed' the wires. He put on a pair of headphones and listened.

There was a lot of buzzing on the wires, the sound of wind and, he thought, of deep breathing. Somewhere in the distance a gramophone was playing. Then he heard the bell ringing. Someone picked up the phone at the other end and there was a muffle of voices. The line was not clear. First there was a man's voice:

'Is that you, Faustina?'

'Yes, darling . . .'

Buzz, buzz, buzz, went the line. Kwaku could only hear snatches of conversation. Then he nearly dropped off the tree in excitement. 'The great robbery . . .' he heard, then, 'meet me at the junction . . . We will share . . . yes, yes, the others will be there, we will all meet in town . . . I will show you the place . . .' Buzz, buzz, buzz, went the line again. Then there was silence and the old sound of wind and crackling.

Hurriedly Kwaku put his tools in the bag. He nearly slipped as he climbed down and almost ran through the coming dark to the village. He went straight to the police station.

'Adamu!' he called, 'Adamu!'

Adamu had closed for the day and was sitting eating stew with his wife. Mariama was feeding the boys in a corner. Adamu wiped his mouth and asked Kwaku what had happened to make him so out of breath. He went on eating while Kwaku talked. At last he put down the bowl and wiped his mouth again.

'So, you think you have found the robbers and you want me to chase them? And how did you, Kwaku Hoampam, get to hear of the phone conversation?'

Kwaku had forgotten that he too had broken the law. For a moment he was confused but his mind worked quickly.

'You know me,' he said. 'I just happened to be outside the box and on hearing the word "robbery" I could not help listening.' Adamu looked at his friend, sighed and commented: 'Eh! Kwaku, you are like the smell of onions, everywhere at once.'

He got up and went into the house and came out in his uniform cap, buttoning up his jacket. 'Come on,' he said. 'If we go now we will catch the girl before she leaves—and maybe we can follow her.'

Together they went out into the street and made their way to the post office. Kwaku dropped his bag at the store as he went past and told them he would be back late. Faustina was just coming out of her door when they reached the house. As soon as she had gone a little way they turned and followed her along the road. She made straight for the junction.

When they came to the bend Kwaku whispered to Adamu and they took the path by the telegraph poles. Adamu followed Kwaku who seemed to be able to see like a cat in the dark. 'Mind the pool on your right,' he whispered. 'The rest is dry just now.'

They arrived at the junction, Adamu puffing a bit but Kwaku too excited to be bothered by the exertion. They waited by the bus stop. Presently a young man got off the bus from the city and crossed the road. Soon after, Faustina came hurrying along the road from the village. She saw the policeman and Kwaku talking by the bus stop and made signs to the young man—which they did not miss. She came straight to talk to them and said she was going into town to see her friends for the evening. She asked them, laughing, if they were out to catch a thief.

'Maybe,' said Kwaku. When Faustina climbed onto the bus the young man followed her and sat by her side. Adamu thought it wiser for him to sit at the back in case they got off in a hurry. Soon Faustina forgot all about them and was chatting cheerfully to the young man.

The lights of town approached. The bus stopped more often and people got on and off. At last it stopped outside the big cinema and Faustina and the young man climbed off. Kwaku and Adamu waited till the last moment and then followed.

'They can't be meeting here!' said Kwaku. 'It is far too public.'

But Faustina and the young man joined the queue for seats. Adamu had time to look around. On the board in front of the cinema was written in large letters: *The Great Robbery*. At first he was angry with both Kwaku and with himself for having been so easily taken in. Then he saw the humour of the situation.

'Friend Kwaku,' he said, 'I am off duty and you are

taking me to the cinema—to the most expensive seats, mind. The film is called *The Great Robbery*. It should be interesting, should it not?'

'You mean?' faltered Kwaku.

'Exactly!' replied Adamu. 'The young lady was making an assignation with her boy-friend. Whether her mother knows of it or not is her own business. I don't think they will have any time for other meetings.'

'Then let's go home,' said Kwaku, hopefully.

'No. It's a long time since I saw a film. I can't afford it often on my pay. You owe me. You will pay, will you not?'

Kwaku grudgingly took the money from the pocket of his shorts. 'That's what comes from trying to be conscientious,' he said. But a little something at the back of his mind kept repeating 'and interfering in other people's affairs.' He soon silenced this voice but he promised himself he would not try and listen in to the telephone again.

The film itself was exciting. Their own robbery had occupied their minds for some days but this was a bigger and better one. A bunch of crooks somewhere in the world had robbed a bank and got away with one million pounds. They were caught, of course, but they nearly got away with it.

'The trouble with us,' said Kwaku, 'is that we don't think big enough!'

After the film Faustina saw them and hurried over. 'Can you take me home?' she asked. 'I did not know you were going to the cinema. I missed my friends.' All the way back they talked of the film.

Adamu's wife was waiting for them. 'Did you catch the thieves?' she asked.

Adamu laughed. 'No, they got away!' but he refused to say any more. Kwaku had to knock on his own door. His son came to open it.

'Eh! you are late,' he said. But in his house no one asked any questions. His wife was fast asleep.

9 *Kwaku Makes a Discovery*

The fact remained that the blue car had not been found. The money was still missing and the robbers at large. Kwaku was relieved that Adamu did not make much of his mistake. Apart from a twinkle in his eye he did not refer to the episode again. Life continued quietly. Kwaku's son's second wife brought forth another daughter, some of the children had measles and his nephews reported that the cocoa had bad black-pod.

Kwaku decided to visit the farm and see for himself. The farm was some way from the village so he started off early in the morning. The dew dripped from the trees and the ground was damp underfoot. He went as far as the bend in the road and turned along a track into the forest. To his surprise he saw the marks of tyres in the soft mud in a hollow.

'That's funny,' he thought. 'I did not know anyone drove along here—not since the timber people left.'

The tracks went on for almost a mile, showing here and there in the mud. Then something blue showed up ahead through the trees. Kwaku quickened his steps, expecting to see someone working on the farm. Soon he came upon the back of a blue Peugeot car. The car was tilted and one tyre was quite flat.

Kwaku walked all round his excitement growing. He tried to remember the number of the missing car and slowly worked out the writing on the number plate—AB 4527—surely that was the missing number?

He stood and listened. There was no one about. Every so often there were small explosions, like guns in the distance, as the plants of 'Ashanti Guns' or 'Old Woman Smoke Tobacco' shot their pollen into the air. There was the rustling and chirruping of insects, but behind was silence. The car had obviously been standing for some days for the boot was already half-covered with fallen leaves. A lizard scuttled across the roof. The windows were opened and the inside was damp. An old sack lay on the back seat.

The visit to the farm would have to wait for another day. Kwaku turned and hurried back along the track. As he went he pictured the headlines in the papers. How he wished that he could read: 'Kwaku Hoampam finds missing car!' or perhaps, 'Great Discovery by Ashanti Farmer'. He quickened his steps.

Adamu was in the office. He looked up in surprise when Kwaku burst in, out of breath with exertion and excitement.

'Good morning,' he said. 'What brings you here in such a hurry? Have you made another discovery?'

'I have found the car!' panted Kwaku.

'Come off it!' laughed Adamu.

'No, it's true. You must believe me. AB 4527 – the blue car. It's in the forest . . .'

'And how would it get there?'

'Along the track to my farm.'

'You must be imagining things,' said Adamu.

Then he looked at Kwaku's face and saw that he was really serious. 'Very well, tell me all about it,' – and he sat back to listen.

When Kwaku had finished his story of the finding of the car Adamu searched through the pile of papers on his desk and found the newspaper report on the robbery. Sure enough it was AB 4527 that was missing.

'This time I think you have something,' he said. 'I will phone headquarters.'

Kwegir Bruce was having his breakfast so it was some time before Adamu managed to speak to the exchange. When he finally got through to the police headquarters it took still longer before he got the right person. Then he began his report. The voice at the other end, which had started by being heavy and formal, grew excited. Instructions were rapped out and as soon as Adamu put down the receiver he started to do up his belt.

'Come on,' he said. 'We are to meet them at the entrance to the track.'

Kwaku hesitated, but not for long. 'I'll just go and tell the family I shall be back for lunch,' he said.

'Be quick then, and mind you don't tell a soul about the car, or all the village will be upon us and the traces will be lost.'

Kwaku was disappointed. He had wanted to be the first to take the news to the village, but he saw the point of Adamu's warning. He hurried home, told them he was not going to the farm after all, as Adamu wanted him to do something, and went down to the bridge where Adamu waited impatiently.

'We shall be there long before them,' complained Kwaku.

'Yes, but now we know, we must see that no one else uses the path.' Kwaku remembered the leaves on the car and the silence of the forest, but he did not say anything

They sat for about half an hour by the road side. It was growing hot and Adamu mopped his face and undid his top buttons. The blue uniform reflected the heat. Lorries and tro-tro cars passed along the road and some of the passengers waved at Kwaku and the policeman, wondering what they were doing there by the roadside. One driver even drew up and asked if he could give them a lift but they explained they were waiting for someone and he did not like to ask more.

At last, the police car came in sight and drew up by the side of the road. A police officer got out and Adamu, hastily doing up his buttons again, saluted. The officer looked at the entrance to the track and tested the ground underfoot.

'I think we had better drive in,' he said, 'just a little way as otherwise people might become curious. We don't want anyone about yet.' So the police driver drove some way along the track until the car was hidden from the road by a bend. Then everyone climbed out. There was a photographer, a man with a notebook and a measure and the driver who locked up the car before leaving it. They went in pairs along the track, Kwaku leading the way with the police officer. Every so often they stopped to look at the marks on the ground. 'It's lucky there has been no rain recently,' said the officer.

After a bit Kwaku stopped and put his hand on the officer's arm. 'There you are,' he said, 'in front through the trees.' Sure enough there was the patch of blue. The officer quickened his steps. The car came in sight.

'Wait!' he said, 'wait until I have looked round.' Then he looked down at Kwaku's sandals and the imprint where he had stood on the damp earth. 'You have already walked around a good deal. I hope you did not touch the car?'

'No,' said Kwaku, grateful that he had been in too much of a hurry to search inside the car. 'I only looked through the windows. I know better than to interfere.'

For about half an hour the officer looked around. Photographs and measurements were taken and inch by inch the whole car was studied for clues. The heat grew, even in the forest, and the flies buzzed round the heads of the policemen. The driver was at last asked to change the tyre so that the car could be driven out. The key was missing but by fiddling about in the engine, the driver made a connection and finally the car jerked into movement. The track was too narrow to turn and they had to find a level place and beat back the undergrowth before it could be eased round. The driver went at a snail's pace through the forest and the officer climbed in beside him, but the others had to walk.

At last they reached the police car, which the driver was forced to back as far as the main road. 'You'd better bring the Peugeot and I'll drive the police car,' the officer told him, then he turned to Adamu. 'You'll be wanted to make a statement, you had better come with me.' To Kwaku he said: 'Sergeant Lafia will take your statement later in the day. We shall want it as full as possible.' Then he climbed into the car.

'Tell my wife I shall be back late,' whispered Adamu, and Kwaku turned back towards the village as the two cars drove off in the opposite direction towards the city.

Left alone on the road, Kwaku walked slowly home.

His wife was in the shop unpacking a new parcel of cloth which had come on one of the early-morning lorries. She looked up: 'So you did not go to the farm after all, Kwasi will be disappointed. What happened?'

'As a matter of fact I was helping the police.'

'The police? What has happened? Is anyone in trouble?'

'No, it's not that. I found the blue car.'

Akosua's mind had been busy with things other than the robbery and she had almost forgotten about it. It had nothing to do with her. She looked puzzled. 'What blue car?' she asked.

Kwaku felt a bit deflated. He had expected that his statement would cause at least surprise, perhaps admiration.

'Eh! you, don't you ever mind what is going on? Surely you remember the robbery last week, and the blue Peugeot?'

'Oh! that one. Well what about it?'

Kwaku, who longed to tell someone of his find and

knew that his wife, at least, could be trusted not to repeat the story, leant against the counter in the store and recounted the whole adventure.

'Well, well,' said Akosua, at last. 'Just to think it was you who found it. Is there a reward?'

'I don't know,' said Kwaku, 'I did not ask. But, listen, wife, I have been told to keep quiet about it until the police are ready to ask questions.'

'Of course,' replied his wife. 'Lunch is nearly ready. I will get the girls to beat the fou-fou.'

Neither Akosua nor Kwaku mentioned the adventure to their neighbours. Nevertheless, by the time Adamu returned in the evening, the whole village was discussing it. Kwaku had missed his chance of being the first to tell the tale and Adamu looked at him accusingly.

'I told you not to tell,' he said.

'I didn't,' said Kwaku.

'Then how do they all know?' asked Adamu.

'I've no idea,' replied a disgruntled Kwaku.

They never found out that one of the policemen was a friend of Faustina's boy friend. The news had come over the phone from headquarters, but Adamu always suspected that Kwaku had given way to temptation and told the story himself.

10 *Catching a Thief*

Kwaku was not, however, quite without honour in his own village. The story was known, it is true, but nothing could take the place of a first-hand account and was it not Kwaku Hoampam, their own Kwaku, who had found the car?

When he went up the village in the evening, there was quite a crowd in the square. Nana Ababio called him into the Ahenfie and made a place for him, others crowded in as best they could and Kwaku told his story.

He made it as dramatic as he could: 'I wondered if the robbers were still there? I listened and listened but only the hornbill cried from the forest. Leaves had covered the roof and bonnet. Then I knew the car had been left alone for a long time.'

'Did you go inside?' asked Kwadwo Amankwa, youngest of the brothers.

'Of course not, I knew the police don't like you to touch anything.'

When the story was finished and Kwaku had been questioned and cross-questioned, the villagers began to discuss the finding of the car. There was a bit of a disturbance at the door of the Ahenfie and Kofi Ampim appeared with a large black pot, which he put down in front of the chief. Soon the calabash was being passed round and the discussion continued.

At first the villagers all said that the car must have been left by a stranger, but as they went into it more deeply, they knew that it could only have been left by someone who knew the forest well. The track was well hidden and only a local man would know how far it led into the forest.

'Why did he stop just there?' asked Kofi Amankwa.

Kwaku thought. 'The track narrows and comes to a stream. There is no bridge.'

'Only a local man would know that.'

'Then it must be one of us,' said someone, laughing uncomfortably. There was angry silence.

Nana Ababio spoke. 'It is up to us to clear our name. Each one of you must think hard as to who would have done such a thing. Who has suddenly found money? Who can drive a car? The culprit must be found.'

'Aye, Nana,' replied everyone.

'Where does the track lead to?—the other end I mean?' asked a young man.

'To the village of Opepease.'

'Then the men might have come from there!'

'There can't be more than ten families in Opepease, including the Odikro. At any rate they seldom use that way now that they have their own road to Bonsua,' commented Kofi Ampim. 'I am surprised that the track is still so clear.'

Next day the discussion was taken up by the old women of the village. They had known most of the other villagers as children, had watched them grow up and knew what they were like. One day a money-doubler had come to the village. The old women had watched and listened and betted on who would fall for his patter. They too in their youth had been tempted. When Kofi, the catechist's brother, lost ten pounds—all his savings—they were not surprised. They remembered him as a child, his eyes wide open as he listened to their stories, believing every bit of them. How he had admired the cunning of Ananse. How he had searched for beads at the end of the rainbow, running along the forest road in his efforts to catch up with it.

Now they turned their minds to finding potential thieves. Isaka Bondo had often been caught stealing small things as a child, but usually to fill his perpetually empty stomach. Yaw Nkrumah had never been able to tell the truth and his stories had bordered on the fantastic. Kofi Ntem was always a quiet child and one never knew what went on inside him, but he was kind to the little ones and would never use violence. When you came to think of it, the possibilities narrowed down to a few men and most of these could be accounted for on the day in question.

The woman gave a sigh of relief and went to inform Nana Ababio that in their opinion it could be no one from the village. Nana Ababio listened to the old women, for he found they were seldom wrong in their judgement of character, unless it was of someone who deliberately contravened custom or who disregarded the older generation. Such characters were at any rate unstable and might always do something bad as they had lost their roots.

The two or three young men who came under suspicion were quickly cleared as they had all been in company at the time. Nana Ababio decided to consult the Odikro of Opepease and a messenger was sent along the forest path to call him.

The Odikro of Opepease was a young man, scarcely more than a schoolboy, but he had inherited from his uncle who had been a man of wisdom, and he had benefited from his instructions. Nana Ababio treated him with courtesy and diplomacy and they were soon discussing village affairs. Nana himself knew quite a few people from Opepease and in particular one of the old women who was considered a witch. Mammy Awuraa Ama had lived in the village until she married her second husband, a man from Opepease. Even in those days she had quite a reputation and people believed that she had deliberately killed her first husband who had had a roving eye. He died in a shooting accident but it was universally believed that witchcraft was involved. Later, when two of her daughters had died, people shook their heads and said that she had killed them out of jealousy. One had married an up-and-coming young man from town and had put on superior airs. Now no one willingly crossed the old woman.

Nana Ababio suggested tactfully that she should be consulted on this matter, together with the other elderly people. The Odikro talked at length about the men of his generation. In such a small village there was not much choice. Then he remembered that one of the young men had returned recently after a long absence. No one knew why he had come back from town, nor why he offered to help his uncle on the farm, since he knew little about farming and cared even less.

'Find out about him,' said Nana Ababio.

So in Opepease the matter was also discussed in detail, though voices grew silent when the prodigal son was present. His name was Kwadwo Oware and he was light-coloured with almost red hair, taking after his mother and his grandmother who had both been red-haired. He used to spend the evenings drinking palm wine but recently he had hardly been in the village. He had new cloths and trousers and seldom went to the farm with his uncle, finding some excuse to loll about the village, a cigarette hanging from the side of his mouth.

One evening, the Odikro called Kwadwo Oware. He asked him to go with him to visit Nana Ababio with some other young men from the village. Kwadwo Oware was reluctant but he did not like to refuse. The Odikro briefed the other young men carefully.

Early on Sunday morning they left Opepease, so that they could go to church in the bigger village—theirs was too small to have even a rough chapel. It was decided to take the forest path although Kwadwo Oware tried hard to dissuade them.

As they came to the slope which led down to the stream,

Kwadwo Oware lagged behind. 'Hurry up!' said one of the other young men, holding him firmly by the arm and pushing him ahead of the group as they splashed through the water and climbed the hill. Soon they came to the spot where the blue car had stood and the Odikro turned suddenly to Kwadwo Oware. 'Where is the car?' he asked.

'Someone must have moved it,' replied Kwadwo and then he realised his mistake. The young men closed round him on the path.

'I think you had better tell us everything,' said the Odikro.

'I don't know what you mean, Nana.'

'Then how did you know there was a car here?'

'I saw it on my way through the forest.'

'When did you come here?'

'Last week.'

'Why didn't you tell us about the car? You knew we were looking for it.'

So the questioning continued.

Kwadwo Oware grew angry. 'Why are you doing this to me? What business is it of yours anyway?' and he tried to push the young men away. They held him firmly and one of them went to cut a thorned stick from the bush.

'You had better tell us everything,' he threatened.

Kwadwo Oware stood irresolute on the path. The young man made a move towards him with the stick. Then he broke down and told them all. He had been in prison in the South and had come home penniless and with little prospect of getting work. One of the men who had been in prison with him had met him in the city and asked him to do a job for him. At first it had seemed straight forward but one thing had led to another and he had become the driver for a small gang of thieves. This was their first big job and they had chosen this area because they knew he would know how to hide the car. The car itself they had easily stolen outside a cinema in Accra, and hidden in the forest until it was ready for the job.

'How much did they pay you?' asked the Odikro.

Kwadwo Oware hesitated, wondering if he should speak the truth. 'About £200,' he said—he had really received £300 but hoped to save at least a small amount out of the disaster.

The Odikro thought for a moment. 'Give me the key of your room,' he ordered. Kwadwo Oware handed it over. Some of the young men were despatched back to Opepease and the rest of the party went on to the village, the young men walking close to Kwadwo Oware. It was about 8.30 when they reached the police station.

Adamu was in his house and they called on him to open the office. He came, grumbling: 'I hope you're not troubling me for nothing,' and, 'Can't a man even have a Sunday to himself?' He opened up the office, sat down at his desk and got out his note book. 'Now?' he said.

'This man has a statement to make,' said the Odikro. 'It is he who stole the blue Peugeot.'

Adamu looked hard at the man in front of him. Kwadwo Oware shuffled his feet and bent his head.

'How do you know? Who is he?' asked Adamu.

'His name is Kwadwo Oware and he comes from Opepease. He has admitted to the crime.'

'They forced me,' said Kwadwo Oware.

'Is it true?'

'Well, in a manner of speaking, it happened like this . . .' and Kwadwo Oware repeated the story he had told to the young men of Opepease.

If Kwadwo Oware had thought he could hide anything, he now knew he was wrong. Step by step, question by question, Adamu squeezed the whole story out of him. Only when he was asked the names of his accomplices did he hesitate. Adamu looked at him.

'Listen,' he said, 'I am not a young man and I have

much experience of life. I know many men in many places. You are not clever enough to tell convincing lies. You had better stick to the truth. If you help the police your sentence is likely to be less and your stay in the cells more comfortable. You are protected by the law, I know, but within the law there are many ways of making things uncomfortable for you. Make a full statement now—the truth, the whole truth and nothing but the truth, and you will avoid much trouble later.'

Kwadwo still hesitated. But Adamu was an experienced man, he had had to deal with many criminals. He loosened the belt on his uniform, judging the reaction of Kwadwo. Kwadwo looked at the belt, not knowing that Adamu would never use it. Adamu swung the belt and let it smack against his thigh as he stood up.

'Heh, wait a minute,' squealed Kwadwo. 'I did not say I would not tell you, now did I?'—and he gave him the names and addresses of his four accomplices.

Adamu sent one of the young men to find the postmaster and to ask him to man the exchange. Presently the phone rang and Adamu was connected with the Central Police Station in the city. He made a fair copy of Kwadwo Oware's statement, read it over to him and asked him to sign it. The belt still lay on the desk.

The bells had just stopped ringing when the Odikro and his party reached church. Room was made for him in front but the young men had to stand as the church was already full. Two of them had stayed behind with Adamu until he could hand over Kwadwo Oware and his signed statement to the police from the city.

Nana Ababio, sitting in front of the congregation, and Kwaku Hoampam, sitting just behind, wondered why the Odikro had come and what news he had brought with him. The catechist seemed to take longer than ever with his sermon, and the women with their chanting. It was not until the last hymn that a whisper reached those in front that the robber had been caught. The crowd divided for the chief to leave the church and the Odikro of Opepease followed him outside. As if by mutual consent they hurried back to the Ahenfie. The elders soon gathered and the Odikro told his tale. A large pot of palm wine was sent for by Kofi Ampam and the calabash was soon passing round.

The Odikro refused politely to use the cracked glass that was offered him as a concession to his education, and joined with the others. It was not until early evening the young men of Opepease returned home, well fortified by the hospitality of chief and village.

11 *The Trial—Adamu's Triumph*

The next day and for many days to come the police station was always busy. Policemen went back and forth to Opepease and came in to take statements from Kwaku and to fetch Adamu. Apart from that the villagers found occasion to drop in about this or that and to collect the latest bit of news about the case. One of the managers of the Bonsua Timber Company came to see Kwaku and brought with him a calendar, a diary and some tobacco, which Kwaku displayed on the counter of his store.

As time passed the accomplices were rounded up, some of the money was recovered, the driver identified the robbers and inexorably the case had its preliminary hearing in the magistrate's court. The magistrate found that the State had a prima facie case against the accused and they were committed to stand trial before the High Court.

Adamu had informed the villagers that the preliminary hearing would be a mere formal affair since there had been a confession, but when the case came before the High Court and witnesses were called the whole village wanted to attend.

Two lorries were hired and those who could make time to attend travelled in them to the city. The lorries reached the High Court early in the morning, for the villagers were afraid they would not get into court. They had to wait a long time, standing about in excited groups outside the court, as another case was still being heard. Faustina, who had come in with the villagers, slipped quietly away to meet her boy-friend and no one missed her.

The case which was nearing conclusion was a particularly nasty one. A nephew was being tried for murdering his uncle. The old man had been found brutally beaten up in his hut on the cocoa farm. There seemed little doubt that the nephew was guilty. The case was almost finished. The prisoner was in the dock and the judgement was given. Before passing sentence the judge asked the prisoner if he had anything to say.

Suddenly there was a gasp of astonishment in court. The judge hurriedly removed his glasses, polished them and put them back on his nose. People at the back craned forward to see. The prisoner staggered in the dock.

There, in the middle of the court, between judge and prisoner, stood a small deer, its startled face turned towards the dock. There was a moment of complete silence before one of the policemen dived to catch it. Then pandemonium broke out. Chairs were overturned, arms and legs inextricably confused as they sought to capture the deer. By the time the people had sorted themselves out the deer had disappeared, as mysteriously as it had appeared.

The judge, who sat like a surprised owl whilst the storm raged around him, suddenly came to. He beckoned to the court usher who shouted: 'Silence in court.'

'We will proceed,' said His Honour. 'Before I pass judgement . . .'

Then he noticed that the accused was slumped in the chair in the dock.

'Make the prisoner stand,' he said.

'I don't think he can, my lord,' said one of the policemen. 'He's been taken queer, what with his uncle appearing like that.'

'His uncle?'

'Yes, my lord—the deer.'

'Rubbish. His uncle is dead. What has the deer to

do with it? If there was a deer?' he added hastily.

The prisoner pulled himself to his feet. His face was grey and his voice hoarse.

'My lord, I have no more to say. I killed my uncle and he has come for me.' Then he collapsed back onto the chair.

'Very odd. Very odd indeed,' said the Judge. Then he did the unprecedented thing of addressing the court before sentencing the prisoner.

'Let no one think,' he said, 'that the extraordinary event we have just witnessed has affected in any way the course of justice. The sentence I shall give is unaltered,' – and he put on the black cap.

There was a short break as the people concerned in the first case streamed out of court, discussing in an excited manner the appearance of the deer.

The villagers pushed their way in to take the empty benches. Their case, the case of the State versus Kwadwo Oware and others, was called.

The State Attorney who was prosecuting and the lawyer for the defence announced themselves after the charges were read and the case was under way. Kwadwo Oware's uncle, seeing the honour of his family at stake, had employed the best lawyer he could find but he knew that the boy stood no chance of being acquitted as he was pleading 'Guilty', in the hope of a shorter sentence. He wondered sadly how his sister had managed to produce such a rascal and what had gone wrong with the boy's training – it must surely have been the father's fault. He had come to listen to the trial with the Odikro of Opepease who was sorry for the old man.

Although Kwadwo Oware himself had decided to plead 'Guilty' the other accomplices were entering a plea of 'Not Guilty' so the trial was likely to take some days. The villagers settled down to listen.

It would be useless to recount the progress of the whole

trial—it took ten days in all as the police built up their case, brick by brick, against the accused. They had been more thorough than usual in their preparations and Adamu had helped with his careful and meticulous statements and his logical mind.

Kwaku Hoampam was at last called into the witness box to give his report of the finding of the car. He hitched his cloth on his shoulder and climbed into the box and looked round the court. He was determined to make his appearance last as long as possible and he embarked on his story in a leisurely way, explaining about the black-pod on his nephew's farm, about the track to Opepease, the work of the timber company which had cleared the forest some years ago, and finally the events of that historic morning. The judge was visibly bored, and would have liked to hurry Kwaku up, but he had learnt from bitter experience that it is hard to silence an Ashanti when he wants to talk. In the long run, it paid to be patient. The story was at last completed and the lawyer for the defence decided it would be useless to cross-question Kwaku. Much to the latter's disappointment, he was forced to climb down from the box and his hour of glory was over. He was jealous of Adamu who played a far greater part in the trial and comported himself so well that towards the end the judge complimented him on the clearness of his statements and the thoroughness of his work and added: 'I hope that your senior officers will take note of this commendation from the Bench.' Adamu beamed.

When the day for final judgement and sentence arrived the court was crammed. Sentences were heavy as there had been too much robbery recently. Only Kwadwo Oware, despite his previous sentence, got off with a slightly shorter term of imprisonment because he had helped the police. Kwadwo's old uncle looked sadly at his nephew as he was led away and the Odikro was forced to jog his elbow before he turned to leave the court.

Kwaku was invited to the offices of the Bulco Timber Company, where there was a formal presentation of a reward for the finding of the car. Akosua went with him, determined to get her fair share and to see that he was not careless with the money. Photographs were taken and the manager promised to send copies to Kwaku and Nana Ababio who had accompanied him.

As he left the offices Kwaku thought how smart his wife looked with her wig and new cloth. She would come out well in the photo and he was lucky to have such a beautiful wife. He put his hand in his pocket and felt the money. Tomorrow they would go to the market together.

12 *Home to the Village*

It was hardly worth returning home for the night, so Kwaku and Akosua decided to stay with her sister Adwoa Ketua and to see the children. It was not often that both of them visited town together and there was much excitement when they arrived at the family house. Most of the women were down cooking their suppers in the court-yard whilst the children sat and played on the steps leading up to the two storeys above.

After greeting all her relations Mammy Akosua led the way upstairs to the first floor where her sister and family lived. Ama Serwaa was sitting at the table with her school books spread out in front of her and Kofi was lying on his stomach on the floor, reading a much-worn library book. They both jumped up and ran to greet their parents, their mother warmly and their father more formally, as they were a little afraid of him.

Kwaku glanced at the books on the table and wished again that he had had the chance the children now had and that he had learnt to read. He was proud of the children but did not really know how to talk to them as they learnt so many things that he did not know about and knew far less about the farms and country lore with which he was so familiar.

Auntie Adwoa bustled into the room from her bed-room, tying up her headscarf as she came and protesting that they should have told her they were coming so that she could have prepared for them properly. She called to the several small girls playing on the balcony and told them to hurry and clean out the guest room and make the bed. Then she went in herself and scolded them until she saw the work was properly under way. She shouted at one of her nephews to go and buy some beer. Her husband was out somewhere so she sat down to talk to Kwaku and Akosua, sending the children here and there with instructions about the meal.

Beer and minerals were soon brought and they started to discuss the case. They sat in three of the four arm chairs whose hard red plastic covers had seen much wear. There was a crocheted mat on the centre table and a bowl of rather dusty artificial flowers. The small tables had been chipped by the constant running back and forth of children. On the walls were many family photographs. The oldest, of grandmother, showed a distinguished woman sitting straight up in her chair with her two feet firmly planted before her and her kente cloth, rows of beads and gold jewellery indicating that she had held an important place in the community.

Kwaku looked at the photos, asked a few questions about them and promised to send his sister-in-law a copy of the photo that had just been taken of Akosua and himself being presented with the reward.

This started further discussion of the case. The children came and sat quietly listening to the account. Once Kofi asked his father shyly if he had not been afraid that the thieves would come back and catch him in the forest.

'Of course not,' replied his father. 'You know I am never afraid. As a good Ashanti you must grow up to be afraid of nothing. Don't they teach you that at school?' After that Kofi was silent.

Ama Serwaa stood behind her mother and looked at her wig. She bent over and whispered something in her mother's ear and Mammy Akosua smiled and, leaving the others to talk, went with her daughter into the bedroom. By now quite a crowd had collected and Kwaku was holding forth about his adventures.

In the bedroom Mammy Akosua removed her wig and, sitting her daughter in front of the mirror, she tried it on her. Ama Serwaa was enchanted. She looked so grown-up and her mother thought that she too would be a beauty when she was older. She must be careful, for her daughter was nearing the dangerous age. She must remember to talk to her sister and warn her to keep a strict eye on Ama Serwaa and see that she came home in time in the evenings. She readjusted the wig on her own head and they returned to the others. Presently Auntie Adwoa's husband came home and there was another round of greetings. More beer was brought and they sat drinking and talking until supper was nearly ready. The visitors went off to have their baths and the children went to join the others downstairs for the evening meal.

The steep concrete steps looked even steeper in the dim electric light and the fires in the courtyard glowed under the steaming pots. Family groups sat round eating their evening meals and the children quarrelled over the last pieces in the communal dish. The little ones soon fell asleep and the older girls played 'ampe' whilst the boys watched the men playing draughts or took it in turns to use the ware board.

Upstairs the most senior members of the household had their meals and talked.

Meanwhile Adamu, covered in glory from his performance at the trial and from the commendations of his senior officers, had returned to the village in the bus with the other villagers. They all treated him with respect and he felt that his position and authority in the community was assured. It was only a pity that his uniform debarred him from accepting a reward.

It was not until the bus arrived in the village square that it was realised that Faustina was not amongst the passengers. Her father, who had come to meet the bus, asked where she was and no one could remember having seen her during the last stages of the trial. The other young women could only remember that she had slipped off soon after the bus reached town and they had not seen her since.

Kwegir Bruce was worried. He decided to telephone his relations in town. He tried several numbers until finally, in despair, he remembered the girl-friend to whom Faustina so often telephoned. He found the number scribbled on the outside of the phone book and decided to ring.

It was a man's voice which answered the telephone and Kwegir asked politely if he could speak to Faustina. There was a silence at the other end and then giggles. 'Who is it?' said a girl's voice. 'I don't know,' replied the man.

Faustina came to the phone. 'Who is it, please?' she asked. When she realised it was her father it was already too late.

'Where are you?' he demanded. 'Who are you with and why did you not return with the others from the trial? You don't know how troubled your mother has been. We have telephoned all your relations in town and it was only by chance I found this number.'

Faustina, unprepared, did not know what to answer. If she said it was her school-friend's house then her father would ask to talk to her friend. In fact she was alone with her boy-friend and had quite forgotten the time.

'I missed the bus,' she said, 'and I had no money to take a taxi and so I came to try and borrow some from friends. I will come soon.'

'What friends?' asked her father. There was no reply. Then Kwegir Bruce demanded to speak to the man who had first answered the telephone and Faustina reluctantly handed over the phone to him. He smiled at Faustina and politely gave his name and address.

'I am engaged to your daughter,' he said. 'I had meant to come and ask your permission before.'

'What do you mean engaged? Why, I have never even met you and know nothing about you. How did you manage to get to know my daughter well enough to engage her? Where have you been meeting her? I demand an explanation!'

'Certainly,' replied the boy. 'You shall have one and I will come and see you tomorrow. In the meantime I will send Faustina back by taxi,'—and he put the telephone down.

When the taxi arrived an hour later, Kwegir Bruce was standing at the door. Several curious heads looked out of the nearby houses and neighbours strolled along the street. Presently there was the sound of screams and of a stick hitting something hard. No one tried to interfere but it was noticed, in the morning, that Faustina limped when she went to fetch water and had some difficulty in bending to the tap. Her eyes were swollen and she hardly greeted anyone. The village wondered what would happen next.

But the young man was no fool. He took a day off work and went to fetch some senior members of his family. His parents were in Accra so he had to content himself with more remote relations. He was persuasive and polite and he explained that his interest in the girl was a serious one and that he would like to marry her when she had finished school. He knew enough about her family to convince his relations that it was a respectable one and they promised to talk it over with Kwegir Bruce. At any rate they owed him an explanation. They severely reprimanded the young man for his failure to consult his family before getting involved, but nonetheless they agreed to go out with him to the village.

Kwegir Bruce had been prepared to deal with a young man on his own. Instead he was faced with four elderly respectable citizens, and a young man standing humbly behind them. He had to invite them into his house and offer the usual polite conversation before they got down to business. The young man looked round for Faustina but she had been told to stay in her room and, remembering her beating, dared not disobey. She would have to rely on her mother to report what happened.

They talked for a long time and exchanged information about families, the boy's prospects and education, Faustina's schooling and the possibility of making a match of it. Both sides decided to consider the matter. The young man was severely reprimanded by all and the young people were forbidden to see each other until a decision was taken. The young man was sent out to buy beer and Faustina's mother went to fetch her to introduce her to the relations. They stared at each other, made a few polite remarks and then she was sent back to her room. When the young man brought the beer, it was poured out. The relations promised to discuss the matter with his parents in Accra and to keep in touch. They said goodbye politely and left for the city.

As soon as they had gone Faustina's parents called her in. They told her that she must remain in the village until she went back to school and that the shool authorities would be warned to keep an eye on her. Faustina wept bitterly at this and said it was not fair to penalise her at school. Both parents tried to silence her by saying that there was a chance a marriage could be arranged.

Faustina, herself, had never thought very seriously about marriage but now found herself committed to it or nothing and she began to turn over in her mind all the things she knew and had heard about her boy-friend. She wondered if he would make a good husband, but had no experience to judge by. She decided to wait and see what happened and to try and please her father so that he would not keep her tied to the house. For a time she was a dutiful daughter and no father could have complained of her—she was humble, obedient and did her best to please.

Writing a story is like the weaving of a mat. At the finish the ends need tidying off, but they are only in reality cut short. Before and after each thread there is the possibility of a never-ending yarn. If the people are real one can at best make a random choice of the events in their lives. This is the story of the life of a village, so in a sense it has no beginning or end. Life is not a tidy affair; where one puts down the load another picks it up.

You, yourselves, know many of the people who have passed by the store of Kwaku Hoampam. Like the smell of onions he may be found in most villages in Ashanti. You often meet Akosua in the market or see Faustina laughing inside the city hotel. The solid figure of Adamu Lafia can be met on many roads. As for the dozens of children that run in and out of the village compounds, you have only to pause to hear them shouting outside.

It is evening now. The rains have come and all good people will be going early to bed. The doors close, the small lights go out, one by one. There is suppressed laughter and hidden tears, and outside it all the thundering of water on metal roofs. You who are inside may go on with the story but we others are tired and must go home.

Firebrands

Sahle Sellassie

A tale of two brothers in the Ethiopia of the early 1970s. Bezuneh, the elder, is a gentle giant of a man, honest and hard-working in a corrupt world. Worku, the younger, is a hot-headed student, eager to sweep away the system and set the downtrodden masses free.

As the people's resentment against their overlords seethes and festers, Bezuneh reaches his own boiling point when he is unjustly sacked. Imprisoned for his murderous assault upon his boss, he is freed after the revolution has overthrown the ruling class. But how far has the system *really* changed?

Sahle Sellassie's third novel is a forceful and realistic story set against the background of the dramatic events of 1974.

ISBN 0 582 64243 4

Muriel at Metropolitan

Miriam Tlali

Muriel is a Black South African who gets a job at Metropolitan Radio, a furniture store in the heart of Johannesburg. Unwillingly she finds herself taking part in the exploitation of her own people, the Black customers who are tempted by 'buy now pay later' bargains and then threatened when they fall behind.

Muriel's personal narrative of day to day life in the store reveals her growing resentment of the petty snubs and indignities unthinkingly dealt out by the white staff. Gradually we come to recognise that the store is a virtual microcosm of South African society under apartheid.

Miriam Tlali's novel, based on her own experiences, describes simply and without sensationalism the plight of the South African Black struggling to find and keep a place in a society where white is always right.

ISBN 0 582 64232 9

Violence

Festus Iyayi

The worst thing that can happen to a man is to wake up each morning not only hungry but with no means of satisfying his hunger or that of his wife. Idemudia's unremitting struggle for survival in a city offering cruel contrasts between direst poverty and ostentatious wealth almost destroys him, his health and his marriage. The bond between him and his wife Adisa is stretched, strained, battered and betrayed, yet from their sufferings miraculously emerge a deeper insight and a closer unity.

This is Festus Iyayi's first novel, written from his own observations of conditions existing in his native Nigeria.

ISBN 0 582 64247 7

Bukom

Bill Marshall

Everyone in Ataa Kojo's family had a different dream. The old man would die happy if only he had a whiteman's toilet installed in his house. His married daughter Karley wanted her husband to be faithful to her, while her young sister Fofo longed for a lover. Of the three sons, Martey the eldest simply wanted more money, Allotey was eager for independence, and the youngest, Chico, desperately needed a kente cloth to wear at the school Speech Day.

How they all set about achieving these ambitions makes a lively, lighthearted story lavishly endowed with colourful Ghanaian atmosphere. Bill Marshall knows Accra's Bukom district well and describes it with humour and affection.

ISBN o 582 64223 x

In the Castle of my Skin

George Lamming

A boy grows up on a small Caribbean island in the 1930s: a personal, partly autobiographical record of adolescence and, at the same time, a record of the pattern of life during a period of rapid social change. The record is earthy, funny, tender, the bright joys of youth contrasted with the darker undertones of helplessness.

First published more than quarter of a century ago, and quickly established as a classic, George Lamming's first novel won many awards and much critical acclaim:

'One is back in the world of Huckleberry Finn. . . . Mr Lamming catches the myth-dissolving mind of boyhood.'
The New Statesman

'Humour, pride, poetry and violence are the qualities that blend in this haphazard yet deeply coherent book.'
The Observer

'There is not a stock figure in the story. Nor is there a trace of the bitter recrimination that stifles many similar books.'
The Sunday Times

'A rich and memorable feat of imaginative interpretation.'
The Spectator

Not for sale in the United States of America, Canada and the Philippine Islands.

ISBN 0 582 64267 1

The Lonely Londoners

Samuel Selvon

In the hopeful aftermath of the war they flocked to the Mother Country: waves of West Indians looking for a prosperous new future and finding instead a cool reception, bone-chilling weather and bleak prospects. Yet friendships flourish among these lonely Londoners and they learn to survive, and even to love their London.

Samuel Selvon's classic novel about immigrants in the 1950s is rich in characters such as Galahad who never feels the cold, Big City who dreams of fame and fortune, Harris who likes to play ladeda, Moses who hates his own soft heart, and the Captain who has a way with women.

ISBN 0 582 64264 7

Jingala

Legson Kayira

Like most Malawian fathers, Jingala believed his word was law. He had only one son, Gregory, of whom he was possessively proud. He was paying for Gregory to be educated by the white men at the Roman Catholic school, but naturally he took it for granted that Gregory would come home and work for him.

So when he heard Gregory was determined to become a priest and the white men were actually encouraging him to disobey his father, he was shocked, appalled, incredulous – and firmly resolved to put a stop to such an outrageous notion.

Legson Kayira's novel takes a fresh look at the age-old theme of conflict between old and young, tradition and innovation, authority and ambition.

ISBN o 582 64268 x

Ways of Sunlight

Samuel Selvon

In these short stories, some set in the Caribbean, some in London, we meet a variety of characters such as Ma Procop, who goes to extraordinary lengths to protect her mango tree; Eraser the bus conductor who loves his bus as a sailor does his ship; Algernon who convinces the English he is an expert on cricket; Small Change who finally wears out the patience of London Transport; and four Jamaican boys who bring obeah to defeat a rapacious London landlady.

When *Ways of Sunlight* was first published, it won high praise from the critics:

'A delightful book. For humour, sprightliness and down-right exuberance at being alive, Mr Selvon's people are positively Neapolitan.'   *The Sunday Times*

'Samuel Selvon brings out well the colour and individuality of life in the West Indies and paints an even livelier picture of exiled West Indians living in London.'
The Guardian

'Mr Selvon writes naturally in dialogue, he never lets the pace sag, and he suggests a scene with a telling economy of means.'   *Times Literary Supplement*

ISBN 0 582 64261 2

A Brighter Sun

Samuel Selvon

Tiger is sixteen. According to custom among the East Indians of Chaguanas, it is time to prove himself a man, to marry a girl he has never seen, to set up his own home, found his own family and earn his own living. Urmilla, his child-bride, shy and bewildered, is equally anxious to prove herself a woman, a wife and a mother.

The setting for this sensitive novel is Trinidad in the years of the second world war, a period of change as intense and far-reaching for Trinidad as the years of his maturing are for Tiger.

Samuel Selvon, himself an Indian from Trinidad, wrote *A Brighter Sun*, his first novel, in 1952; it is now established as a classic.

ISBN 0 582 64265 5

Edufa

Efua T. Sutherland

For a successful, modern, educated Ghanaian, Edufa is surprisingly insecure. He has partially deserted the values of the African society into which he was born, and in his passion for status and prestige he is driven to barter his beloved wife's life against loss of these privileges. But he is not prepared for the day of reckoning . . .

This early play by Efua T. Sutherland, first published in 1967, shows the playwright's command of tragic drama as well as her sympathetic understanding of human failings and frailties.

ISBN 0 582 64272 8

No Sweetness Here

Ama Ata Aidoo

Eleven short stories, with themes as diverse as they are universal in appeal illustrate the author's keen awareness of the conflicts and confusions in post-colonial Ghana, Among the characters she creates are the bewildered black servant no longer sure of his role; two sisters, the elder shocked by the brazen behaviour of the younger; a heedless child who is the bane of her mother's life until the day she attempts a selfless action; the lonely mother who tragically loses her only child.

Well known as a playwright and more recently as a novelist, Ama Ata Aidoo has turned her storytelling skill to the difficult art of the short story with assured success.

ISBN 0 582 64271 X

Not for sale in the USA and Canada